Get Your
Coventry Romances
Home Subscription NOW

And Get These
4 Best-Selling Novels
FREE:

LACEY
by Claudette Williams

THE ROMANTIC WIDOW
by Mollie Chappell

HELENE
by Leonora Blythe

THE HEARTBREAK TRIANGLE
by Nora Hampton

**A Home Subscription! It's the easiest and most convenient way
to get every one of the exciting Coventry Romance Novels!
...And you get 4 of them FREE!**

You pay nothing extra for this convenience; there are no additional
charges...you don't even pay for postage! Fill out and send us the handy
coupon now, and we'll send you 4 exciting Coventry Romance
novels absolutely FREE!

SEND NO MONEY, GET THESE
FOUR BOOKS
FREE!

━━ ━━ ━━ ━━ ━━ ━━ ━━ ━━ ━━ ━━ ━━ ━━ ━━ ━━ ━━

C1080

MAIL THIS COUPON TODAY TO:
COVENTRY HOME
SUBSCRIPTION SERVICE
6 COMMERCIAL STREET
HICKSVILLE, NEW YORK 11801

YES, please start a Coventry Romance Home Subscription in my name,
and send me FREE and without obligation to buy, my 4 Coventry Romances.
If you do not hear from me after I have examined my 4 FREE books, please
send me the 6 new Coventry Romances each month as soon as they come
off the presses. I understand that I will be billed only $10.50 for all 6 books.
There are no shipping and handling nor any other hidden charges. There is
no minimum number of monthly purchases that I have to make. In fact, I can
cancel my subscription at any time. The first 4 FREE books are mine to keep
as a gift, even if I do not buy any additional books.

For added convenience, your monthly subscription may be charged automatically to your credit card.

☐ Master Charge   ☐ Visa

Credit Card #_____

Expiration Date_____

Name_____
                                    (Please Print)
Address_____

City_____State_____Zip _____

Signature_____

☐ Bill Me Direct Each Month

This offer expires March 31, 1981. Prices subject to change without notice
Publisher reserves the right to substitute alternate FREE books. Sales tax collected where required by law. Offer valid for new members only.

ROSE TRELAWNEY

Joan Smith

FAWCETT COVENTRY • NEW YORK

ROSE TRELAWNEY

Published by Fawcett Coventry Books, a unit of CBS
Publications, the Consumer Publishing Division of CBS Inc.

Copyright © 1980 by Joan Smith

ALL RIGHTS RESERVED

ISBN: 0-449-50105-1

Printed in the United States of America

First Fawcett Coventry Printing: October 1980

10 9 8 7 6 5 4 3 2 1

To my daughter, Mimi

Chapter One

Someone is trying to kill me. That much I think is clear now. The attack outside the chapel and the drugged coffee—no accidents or misadventures, but attempts by the same hand to do away with me. Why? Surely of all the harmless people in this great big world, no one could be more harmless than a girl who doesn't even know her own name.

Maybe if I lie still in the dark it will come back to me. 'What's your name?' 'I'm . . .' 'Allow me to introduce Miss . . .' 'Of course you know my daughter . . .' Nothing. Ever since that night in the snow I have been Miss Nobody, or possibly *Mrs.* Nobody, though I have no recollection of a husband or beloved children clinging to me. Surely one would remember such precious possessions, more precious even than a name. Being without a name is no more than an inconvenience, really. It is the lack of a past that bedevils one, and the uncertainty of a future after these 'accidents' that cause the blood to run cold. As cold as the wind that night. How cold it was, but then it was December.

And it was snowing. When I awoke lying in the ditch, there was snow falling on me, soft white flakes, so lovely they looked, each with a little yellowish-blue irridescent halo around it, caused by light striking them from behind. Moving, bobbing lights they were, like two small moons come to earth to frolic down this road. Like a fool I lay cowering silently in my cold ditch and let them go by, those two carriage lights, and felt very cunning doing it, too. Only after the sound of the wheels had receded well into the distance did it occur to me there would have been help in the carriage. I tried to stand up then, to shout after the fast-disappearing shadow, and then I nearly passed out again. Sunk down on to the cold blanket of snow while the world spun around me. Black limbs nude of leaves scarcely visible through the swirling snow began wheeling in crazy circles, becoming fuzzy, then completely invisible as a purple curtain fell over them, then back into focus again, sharply etched in outline now like a charcoal sketch, except that they swayed slightly with an occasional creak as they strained against the trunk.

I felt a sudden compulsion to run as fast as my wobbly legs would carry me, away. But where was away? Was it down the lane after the carriage, or behind me, in the other direction, down the black, empty road? Where was I, and what was I doing here? It did not yet occur to me to ask the other great unanswerable. Who am I?

That came a whole hour later, after I had taken the arbitrary decision to follow the carriage. Actually, I rather enjoyed that walk through the darkness. It was black as pitch, with the white flakes swirling against my face, so I felt safe. No one could see me in the dark. It was necessary that no one see me. I wore a good warm cape with a hood and serviceable woolen gloves, but my feet were numb with no galoshes. For an hour I trudged on, taking great gulps of the cold, clean air, looking behind me and straining my eyes forward through the snow, always with a trembling fear that someone would come. Someone would find me. No one did. After an hour, I had walked roughly four miles, and found myself at a place called Wickey, pop. 324, Winchester, 10 miles. I felt able to walk on the ten miles and see the cathedral, despite the cold.

Wickey had a church of its own. Not a cathedral, but a pretty little building of gray stone with a deeply-recessed doorway. There appeared to be carvings in bas-relief around the arch of the main door, and pillars, in the Norman style. I stood there in the dark admiring what I could see of it, all alone. No one would harm anyone right in front of a church. Why did I have this uneasy feeling someone wanted to? I shook my head. I would sleep in the church. I tried the door, and it didn't move an inch. Locked. Naturally a church would be locked in the dead of night! But they were sometimes left open in Spain and France, the Catholic countries. Never mind, my lady, you're in good old Anglican England now, and it is locked. Well then, get the minister to open it, and let you spend the night on a wooden bench. Pilgrims have done it before in other countries. I peered around to discern a small brick cottage set back to the right of the church, but it had no lights on. The Reverend must be in bed, I thought. I would have to wait till morning. Where should I wait?

I realize now I was in a state of shock. I am not usually so foolish as this past recital would indicate. It took me full ten minutes to come to the conclusion the open street was a poor place to spend a night, in the middle of what turned out to be a blizzard, though it was only beginning then. I decided what I ought to do was go to an inn. I retained that much sense, knew, too, it would look odd for me to go without my woman, but this seemed not to distress me. What did bother me, however, was to find my pockets to let—no money, no sign of a reticule to my name. Nothing, barring the clothes on my back. I looked up and down the deserted street, where no one stirred but myself and a mutt, a mongrel who sniffed twice at my feet, then turned his tail to me and trotted off. The lucky dog seemed to know what he was about. I didn't.

Back to the church. A church was safe—maybe a rectory was safe, too? It was becoming bitterly cold, the wind rising and finding its way under the folds of my cape. I stepped cautiously to the door of the rectory and tapped timidly at the brass knocker. Nothing happened. Why was I standing here shivering while an unfeeling housekeeper slept snugly in her bed? I tapped louder, and still nothing happened. Impatient, I gave the brass knocker a couple of resounding crashes that rattled the door on its hinges. At length a lamp appeared within, jiggling towards me. The inner door was opened by a little lady in a cap and dressing gown, holding her lamp high now, looking through the storm door. She appeared frightened, but when she saw it was a lone female seeking entrance, she undid the lock and stuck her head out.

"What do you want?" she asked.

"I want to come in."

"Who are you?"

"I'm . . ." That's when I discovered I didn't know who I was. Till that moment it had not occurred to me to wonder. I was me, that's all.

"I'm cold," I said, shivering and with my teeth chattering. My voice, she told me later, sounded strange, weak. It incited her to pity, but then Miss Wickey, whose family history was likely wrapped up in the village whose name she bore, was full of pity for everyone. She let me in, built up a hasty fire in the grate, made tea, all without a single question, but only a calming string of inconsequential chitchat about the storm. She was mouse-like, gray, small, twitching nervously. A dear woman. Not till I had had two cups of tea and was warm enough to remove my cape did she repeat the question.

"I didn't catch the name, dear," she said, smiling expectantly.

"I didn't throw it, ma'am," I answered pertly, then giggled. She must have thought me a regular hoyden. What induced me to say such a bold thing, and to this old sweetheart?

"But what is it?" she repeated, unoffended, but looking puzzled.

Then, when I was nice and safe and warm, I dissolved into tears. Suddenly the fear returned. I found myself trembling in front of the fire, with the woman's arms around me, cradling me as though I were a baby. I wanted to stay forever safe and warm in her small arms that didn't go half way around me. I also wanted to run away, and break into sobs, and do I hardly knew what. Kill someone I think, for there was anger rolled up with all my other confused emotions. Outrage perhaps was more like it—a sense of definite outrage about something.

It was in no way directed at Miss Wickey, however. She was my refuge. She got me into a nightdress of her own, much too small of course, scarcely past my knees. She frowned as I removed a very plain navy bombazine gown, well worn, too, to reveal fine silken petticoats, with dainty blue ribbons threaded through a lace flounce, the whole well bespattered with mud from my walk. My hose too were of silk, though my shoes were plain in the extreme, and didn't fit any too well. It was too difficult to think about. I was suddenly exhausted.

"Stay with me," I begged her as I crawled into the spartan little cot, without a canopy or any protection of any kind. She put down the candle and brought a chair to my bedside, sat there by me till I fell into a sleep. It didn't take long.

"Thank you, Kitty," I said, yawning.

"That's Wickey, miss," she replied gently. They were the last words I heard that night.

* * *

By morning the snowfall had turned into a storm of major proportions. I suspect I was a nuisance of the same dimensions in the little rectory. I had a fever, a splitting headache, and a wretched cold. I also had a black hole where a memory should have been. Miss Wickey brought me bread and tea on a tray—such a skimpy little breakfast, I thought. A meal for a prisoner. Where was the hot cocoa, where the freshly-baked baps, the eggs? Why did the cup weigh half a pound, a thick, ugly thing with no adornment on its plain gray glazed exterior? I drank the tea, ate the bread, and slept again, still hungry.

Later she sent the Reverend Mulliner to me. He was a windbag. What is it in the ministry that attracts inveterate rashers of wind? The chance to stand up with a captive audience and prose on forever without interruption, I suppose. One would think a stray woman, straggled in in the middle of the night like a cat, and one who had lost her memory into the bargain would be of sufficient interest that he would care to listen, but no, he talked instead. He had heard my story from his housekeeper, Miss Wickey, he informed me. He stood at my bedside, a tall, dark-haired gentleman in ecclesiastical garb of a very good cut, better than one would expect in the rector of such a small parish. He could not be a man of independent means, living so meagerly, so I surmised he was vain, spending an inordinate amount of his stipend on his wardrobe. He was somewhere in his mid-thirties, not bad-looking but for the air of self-consequence he wore.

"Well, well, so we are honored with a guest today! In the ministry we consider housing the afflicted not only a duty, but an honor, ma'am. 'Whatsoever you do unto the least of my . . .' Not to say you are the least, I'm sure! Heh heh," he apologized as his eyes alit on my silken petticoats drying on the back of a chair. Not before a fire, alas! There was no cosy fire for the afflicted.

"You must not feel because the accommodations are

12

small and the fare humble that the hospitality is strained. Share and share alike." But there was an aroma of bacon seeping through the open door hinting at some unshared victuals, nevertheless. "Many's the time this humble abode has offered shelter to one in trouble. When the late Reverend Wickey was in residence—you met his daughter, my housekeeper—not very capable but a good woman with the parishioners. Ah, as I was saying, when the late rector resided here there was a hostel attached to my little cottage. A wretched ramshackle thing it was of clapboard. It fell down from age. Well, well, and how do you go on?"

"My head is a little . . ."

"I'll have the doctor in. A veritable good Samaritan, our Dr. Fell. Don't worry, he'll bill you. All part of the hospitality, heh heh. The mind is a strange thing. Not the least of God's mysteries. If it is playing this stunt on you, you may be sure there is a reason for it. Such things have happened before, but Fell will sort it out."

He was a roamer. Even in a chamber less than ten feet by ten, he could not stand still. As he preached—and I think he was rehearsing Sunday's sermon featuring himself (not Fell) as the good Samaritan—he roamed, glancing at my cape hung on the closet door, my shoes under the one chair, a faded print of the Last Supper on the wall, the window.

"What a day it is! The McCurdles were right to prophesy a storm. It has snowed for ten hours straight. There's six inches of the stuff outside. There will be no one at the service this morning," he repined.

"Oh, is it Sunday?"

"It is the Lord's Day. The McCurdles will be there, of course. They always can make it, only a hop across the road. All the villagers, in fact, could make it, but folks won't come in from the countryside. There will be less than half a congregation this morning. Sir Ludwig won't attempt it from Granhurst."

"Don't let me detain you, Mr. Mulliner. You will be busy this morning," I said, in an effort to be rid of him.

He smiled a cold smile that tried very hard to be warm, but he was rueing the loss of Sir Ludwig, I think, to his flock that morning. "I shall look in on you after lunch," he threatened, and left, with a last hopeful glance to the silken petticoats. I took the notion he hoped he had a lady of consequence gracing his spare room. It would flatter his self-importance no doubt if I could be found to be an aristocrat or something of the sort.

With less than half a churchful to hear the sermon on the Good Samaritan, Dr. Fell was forced to attend before being allowed to come to me. He entered soon afterwards, carrying a black bag with him. He was an elderly man, fiftyish, stooped in shoulders, with all the kindness and charity that ought to have belonged to the Reverend. He tended first to my physical ills, discovering a bump on the back of my head, a congesting lung, and of course the fever. An ill-tasting draught was ordered, then he drew up a chair and sat down beside me.

"You mustn't let this get you down," he said in a very peaceful tone. "A little lapse of memory is the commonest thing in the world after an accident. A day or two of rest and it will all come back to you. You've had a bump on the head, my dear. Have got a bit of a cold from your walk in the snow as well, but outside of that you're a fine healthy young lady. Not a thing to worry about. Let your folks do the worrying. They'll be wondering what's happened to you. A pity, but you're safe here. Miss Wickey will take good care of you. When this snow lets up they'll be coming after you, very likely, your family. Meanwhile you just have a good rest."

"I can't remember *anything*!" I told him.

"You remember coming here last night."

"Yes, yes. I remember that—I walked for ages in the snow. That's all I remember from my past."

"Well, that's something, isn't it? A pity this storm came along to hold us up, but when it clears we'll take

14

a drive out to the spot where you came to, and it will all come back to you. If it hasn't done so before that. We'll find you descended from a stage, find where it came from, and soon we'll know who you left behind. How do you *feel*?" he asked.

"Scared," I answered, without having to think about it.

He nodded, as though it were the answer he expected. Soon he left, but he had helped. His malodorus draught cleared my head, and his calming presence laid some of my fears to rest. It wasn't an uncommon thing after all to suffer a little loss of memory. It happened all the time. I had probably got off a coach, and been hit by something—a falling branch possibly in that storm, and been knocked unconscious. It seemed almost mundane, until nightfall.

Then as I lay alone in the darkness, it seemed less ordinary. Why should I have got down from a stage in the middle of nowhere? There had been no houses nearby. There had been no one to meet me, either. No one making enquiries as would surely have been done had my contact been late for the appointment. If neither the rector nor his housekeeper nor the doctor recognized me, obviously I was a stranger to the neighborhood. A young lady would not be walking alone in the dark, into a howling storm. She would have a trunk, a case or at least a reticule. She would not be wearing a plain navy bombazine gown and shoes that did not fit her, not with a fancy silken petticoat under her gown at least. She would not have this insurmountable feeling of dread hanging over her—this ominous certainty that someone was after her. She wouldn't be angry as a hornet either, and my anger was as great as my fear.

Chapter Two

The storm continued intermittently for two days,
heaping an unaccustomed ten inches of snow on the
roads, making them impassable. Making a trip to that
spot where my memory began impossible, too. Dr. Fell,
who lived in the village, came once, sometimes twice a
day to cheer me. He allowed me to read and to get out
of bed, but he mercifully kept the curious villagers at
bay. The Misses McCurdle in particular were eager to
meet me. Miss Wickey pointed them out to me on one of
their trips to the door—a pair of hawk-nosed dames
both in black, with garishly-colored feathered chapeaux
atop their heads. Fell explained away my lack of
belongings by assuring me we would find them abandoned on the roadside where I had gained consciousness.
He pointed out that I remembered many things. I told
him, for instance, that I had already read the novels of
Miss Edgeworth, that I liked Dr. Johnson's works but
disliked Walter Scott's. He tried various tricks to make
me regain my memory. He put a pencil and paper in

my hands and told me to write, thinking I suppose that I might write my name. What I wrote instead was 'Help me,' in a shaky scrawl.

Miss Wickey, too, was a frequent visitor. She let me in on the stories going around the village, the little neighborhood gossip. The McCurdles had sent a pair of footboys ploughing down the road through snow to their knees to the spot where I said I had come to, but there was no trunk found, no bag, no reticule. They did not quite castigate me as an outright liar, but the word 'alleged' was being hurled about with regard to my story. This would be pique that I had not allowed them an audience, Wickey told me. It thrilled her that she had access to me; they had not. The spinsters fancied that as I arrived at one, I must have left the spot at around twelve, and had therefore almost certainly descended from the night stage to Winchester. That a decent, Christian woman should be traveling alone in such a manner did much to counteract the glory of the silken petticoats. The stages were not operating these days during the storm, however, and travel of any sort was extremely difficult, so that no enquiries in that regard were instituted. That I was apparently headed east told us I came from the west. We examined together maps, hoping a name would jump out and hit me in the eye. None did.

We discussed my strange outfit. The plain outer wrapping, fancy underpinnings. "Maybe my mistress gave me the petticoats," I suggested.

"They were nearly new, both of them," Miss Wickey countered. "And—and you must not take it amiss, my dear, it is not a dig in the least, but a lady who was in service would make her own bed in the morning. Little things you say and do—well, your hands for one thing, white and unmarked and manicured like a lady's hands. And the quantity of butter and sugar you use—not that I mean to say you should not, but servants would be more sparing."

Here all along I had thought I *was* being sparing,

due to the miniscule quantity of these goods placed on a table for three. I took my meals with Mulliner and Miss Wickey after the second day. Other things unmentioned by Miss Wickey but noticed by myself supported this idea. I found the meals at the rectory inferior almost to the point of inedibility. The wine, too, was scarce and what there was of it execrable, the service intolerable. A dozen times I had been about to ring a bell to summon a servant, only to look around in impatience and find no bell. But if I were such a grand lady as this would indicate, why did I wear bombazine? Why did I travel alone? Why was not my prestigious family out proclaiming my absence?

When I was alone, I looked into the little faded mirror over my washstand, to examine this strange body I wore. My hair was an utter mess. I had no one to dress it for me, and wore it pinned in an unbecoming knob at the back, like Miss Wickey. It was chestnut brown, thick and of medium length, with a natural wave. The eyes too were brown, the face pale—an oval face with an ordinary nose and full lips, teeth in good repair. I didn't even know my age. Not a girl—over twenty, but not old. Between twenty and twenty-five I estimated. I was tall, not ill-formed, but with a little fuller figure than I considered ideal. In a better gown I thought I might possess elegance. I carried myself well, proudly. Even the word arrogant did not seem amiss.

Over the week, the storm passed, the roads were cleared, my cold healed and I found myself a stranger being billeted on a country rector and his long-suffering housekeeper. Enquiries of the stage driver, whose customary route was now open, revealed that he thought someone, possibly a woman, had been let down around the spot where I was first born into this new life. He didn't know where I had got on—not later than Shaftesbury, the last stop, possibly before. Due to the lapse of time and the difficulties caused by the storm, he was extremely vague about it all. Newspapers were scanned in vain for a clue as to my identity, but we did no advertising of our own, thinking every day that it would all come rushing back to me. I made no push to institute any advertisements. I wanted to remain hidden away from whoever might be after me. I wanted to discover who I was, but I had a strong compulsion to do it on my own. 'Fear of the unknown,' Dr. Fell called it.

Mulliner must have abandoned the idea I was a woman of any importance. His manner began to change after about four days, after four visits with the McCurdles that would be. He was now merely tolerant, with even that wearing thin. He sat one night with Dr. Fell and myself in the small study of the rectory discussing what was to be done with me. "Thing to do, I think, call Sir Ludwig," he suggested.

"He's gone to London," Dr. Fell told him.

"Is he so? Odd he didn't tell me," Mulliner answered, miffed. He often mentioned Sir Ludwig, but I had not yet laid eyes on the gentleman.

"Maybe I could work for someone," I suggested.

Mulliner brightened up at this. He had half a dozen boys coming in for lessons in the mornings. If I was to batten myself on him, I could work for my bread, the look said. It was done. For three days the six boys sat under my unwatchful eye in this same study, reading poorly, writing worse, and trying vainly to put together the map of the world. I was amazed at their ignorance of geography. One of them was quite insistent France belonged in Asia, so I described it to him a little, its climate and vegetation.

"Have you been there, miss?" he asked.

"I have read about it, as any educated person has," I answered, frowning. Yet I felt I had done more than read about it. I knew the look and smell of the Seine, knew it in springtime, with the trees in new leaf and the walks crowded with—Englishmen! No, it was a vivid dream, obviously.

"I still say it's in Asia," he insisted. "They moved it at the Congress of Vienna."

I had been explaining a little earlier how the map of

Europe had been altered a few years previously by the Congress. He apparently took my lessons to mean Russia and Prussia had literally 'taken' a piece of this or that country and dragged it off. But France at least had not been so dismembered that it went to England, and those Englishmen I saw jostling along the banks were out of place, a dream. Ah, but they weren't! The *ton* of England had gone to France after Waterloo, gone in droves to see it anew after being rid of Bonaparte at last. 'Now at last we can get to Paris!' Someone was saying it to me—I could hear his voice. Oh speak louder, louder!

"So France goes here," Billie McKay said, shattering the memory, and nearly shattering Mulliner's cardboard map by trying to push France in where it did not belong.

"It's eleven o'clock. Time for 'rithmetic," another said.

Arithmetic! What a loathsome word. Some absolute demon named Wardle had collected a mass of impossible riddles and put them all into a green book to pester us. He added only the meagerest of clues to solve these riddles, too. Three barleycorns make an inch, four inches a hand, twelve inches a foot, and such unhelpful facts. How was one to deduce from that the area of a field shaped like a star? Impossible! No one in all of Great Britain surely possessed such an oddly-shaped field. I doubt one exists in the whole world. We dispensed with Arithmetic that day and read Dr. Johnson instead. Indeed we dispensed with Arithmetic entirely, till Mulliner found out what I was up to.

Little as I knew about my past history, I knew I was not accustomed to receiving a dressing down from such an upstart as this man. My hot blood boiled. He preached to me of duty, when he was dumping his own duty in my lap, and so I told him. It was clear after I called him Jack Dandy that I must leave the rectory, but where to go? The Misses McCurdle, from nothing other than a vulgar sense of curiosity, offered me sanctuary. They thought I might be useful with a needle! I knew where I would jab any needle I held if I had to remain in the same house as that pair of harpies. They finally got in to see me. Mulliner sneaked them in one day I was at lessons with the boys. They took turns staring at me and asking questions: while one pried, the other scrutinized my gown, shoes, hair. It wouldn't have greatly surprised me had they lifted my skirt to get a view of the famous petticoats. I would sooner have scrubbed cutlery or served ale at the local tavern than move in with that pair.

After dinner I went into the saloon to peruse the papers—first for any article relating to myself, then for positions open for women. While at this chore, I heard a caller being announced. Not an unusual occurrence, but when the name Sir Ludwig Kessler was relayed to Mr. Mulliner, my interest perked up. I had heard much of Sir Ludwig during the ten days of my stay here. He was the local god, of more importance to Mulliner than the One above, as he held the living at St. Martin's. I waited for them to enter, that I might see for myself the proud owner of Granhurst, the giver of a living to that old fake Mulliner, and why not a sinecure to Miss Nobody, as he was so rich? Miss Nobody had been christened temporarily Miss Smith, though was much wider known locally as 'that woman.'

Oh yes, I had become the resident freak. Mulliner ought not to have resented my presence. All three hundred and seventy-four of the locals and every farmer's wife for miles around had come with a flitch of bacon or basket of bread to get a look at me. A pity none of them had brought sugar or butter. Mulliner had lately been hoarding them at his own end of the table, and failing to hear any request to pass them. Sir Ludwig was likely here to have a look at me as well, if the truth were known. I decided the price for a glimpse of Lady Lazarus, risen from her dead past, would be a position in his household. I would ask for it outright. I smoothed my hair and prepared an enticing smile, only

22

to see the back of a shoulder being shown into Mulliner's study. That wretch of a rector wasn't going to let me meet Sir Ludwig. Not till he had turned him against me at least. The vanishing shoulder wore a drab great-coat with many collars, denoting a gentleman of fashion. He was tall, dark-haired, and had, mercifully, a nice loud voice. If I sat in the chair next the door, kept my door open and strained my ears, I might be able to overhear their conversation, from which I was being pointedly excluded.

Sir Ludwig's half of it at least was perfectly audible. "What's this I hear about a strange woman having landed herself in your lap?" he asked. 'Strange'? Here was a new description.

Mulliner mumbled some reply, lengthy, of which only a few words reached me. ". . . *trying* to teach . . . wretched muddle of it . . . bossy and overbearing . . ." How I longed to jump up and light into him.

"What does she look like?"

More mumbles. ". . . not *old* exactly . . . strapping girl . . . no reason she can't work . . . eats like a horse . . ."

"How old?"

Not a sound. I expect he hunched his shoulders. Mulliner was a shoulder-huncher.

"Who the devil can she be?"

"Anybody . . . governess' frock . . . silk petticoats . . . probably lying, if the truth were known." I was breathing so hard I could hardly keep my seat. In fact, I couldn't. I jumped up and shook my fist at the door, but the louder voice spoke again.

"What, in some kind of trouble you mean?" As if losing one's memory were not trouble enough!

"Determined she won't be found . . . no move to find . . . McCurdles offered . . ."

"Oh Christ, John, that pair of harpies!" I began to like Sir Ludwig.

"You could always use . . . help you with paperwork . . . maid . . ." But how I loathed Mulliner more with every word he uttered.

"A governess is what I need."

"Oh, governess! She can't add two and two!" That he would say good and loud, pest of a man. ". . . seems well enough read . . ."

"Speak French?"

Mumbles that sound negative. '*Mais oui! Je parle français courramment*! Oh, why had no one asked me that? I could speak French. I was hard pressed to keep from bolting into that study.

"Just the finishing touches. A little French, some drawing lessons, pianoforte. I can get her out of your hair for the time being at least." Delightful phrase! I sounded like a bat. "Poor Wickey must be sleeping in the cheese room. Bring the girl in." My beginning to like Sir Ludwig had been premature. Bring her in—for inspection, like a filly or a heifer. Without wasting a second I dashed up the stairs two at a time. If Sir Ludwig wished to inspect me, he would send word to my room, and I would keep him waiting *at least* five minutes.

Word was brought on the instant. As the servant girl chose to use the phrase 'right away,' Sir Ludwig cooled his heels for ten minutes, not five. When I was good and ready, actually when I could contain my own curiosity no longer, I arose and tripped down the stairs. In his eagerness for a look at me, Sir Ludwig had removed to the hallway, to the very bottom of the staircase, where he stood with one hand on the newel post, the other on his hip, straining his neck up to see me. He had a monocle stuck in one eye, and on his face there rested an expression of the greatest curiosity. It was natural I suppose, yet I had come to resent prying eyes, the curious half smile that accompanied the first examination of me. That look, as though one were for the first time getting a glimpse of a tigress, or an exotic bird from some faraway land.

"So this is your stranger," Sir Ludwig said, turning to Mulliner, after he had stared his fill of me. And this was the great Sir Ludwig—a mannerless country squire despite the many-collared coat. A big, bulky man with all the graces of a hound.

Not even a how do you do, but an offhand comment *about* me, as if I were not present, or not a creature to be acknowledged as an equal. The frustrations of the past days welled up into one giant explosion inside my chest. "Sorry I couldn't provide you with two heads, or five or six legs, to have made your trip worthwhile," I heard myself say. I had the pleasure of seeing Sir Ludwig's monocle drop out of his eye with the shock of my gall. Still it was an evil genie who compelled me to be rude to this man, after tolerating the impertinent questions of so many others. Humankind can bear only so much; my own breaking point is a monocle. A quizzing glass already sets my hackles up, but it at least can be attributed to a love of fashion. There is nothing fashionable about a monocle, and unless a person has impaired vision, in which case he ought to purchase a pair of spectacles, I can see no requirement for a monocle. It is my firm belief it is used for the purpose of intimidation. Very likely some unhappy experience from my forgotten past is responsible for this quirk, but I am stuck with it, and with an utter revulsion for a monocle.

Our visitor's astonishment was rapidly giving way to offense. His black slashes of brows rose, his chin went up, as he first glared at me, then turned a demanding eye to Mulliner, who hunched his shoulders. 'This is what I have had to put up with,' his wounded face implied. "This is the young lady I spoke of," is what he actually said. "We are calling her Miss Smith for the moment."

"Does your friend also have a name, for the time being, Mr. Mulliner?" I asked, to give Kessler a taste of being talked about in his own presence.

"Sir Ludwig Kessler," Mulliner replied, as though he were announcing His Majesty George III, at the very least. Only the blare of trumpets was lacking.

I curtsied, not low, and said, "Pleased to make your

acquaintance, Sir Ludwig. A German name, I take it? You do not look German." I had pictured him a stout, red-faced, blue-eyed Teuton. He more closely resembled a Spaniard grown tall. But it could be the darker coloring of the Alpine Germans with the taller build of the Teutonic branch. The head was long and flat enough, not the short, broad head of the southern Germans. The cheekbones were high, the long nose large but well-sculpted.

He did not bow, offer a hand, or smile. He looked, with his black brows raised to an unnaturally high level over dark eyes, whose shade was indistinguishable in the darkish hallway. After a long examination of my face he replied, "Neither do you."

The remark baffled me, but eventually I assumed he meant I, too, looked un-German. "There is not the least reason to assume *I* am of German extraction," I pointed out.

"No, she's English all right," he said to Mulliner, then turned back to continue his perusal of me. The gown now, or the figure. The figure, in fact. A man's eyes do not linger so long over navy bombazine of an uninteresting cut. No sign of approval escaped his eyes or lips. Just so would a man assess an animal he was considering purchasing. "Do you speak French?" he asked.

"Yes."

"Well?"

"Fluently." I posed him a nice, long, difficult question in French having to do with Goethe. He blinked, without attempting a reply.

"Play the pianoforte?" he fired off next.

"I don't know. There is no instrument here for me to try. Till I try a thing, I don't seem to know whether I can do it."

"Do you sketch, paint?"

"Yes."

"You've tried that, then?"

"No." I frowned as the contrariety of this answer

26

struck me. "But I have been missing my brushes," I said, and it was true. Now I realized what it was that had made the days drag so. I hadn't painted since coming here, and I missed it. I could almost feel a brush between my fingers, smell the pigments, see the canvas stretched white and pristine on its frame.

"Never mentioned it," Mulliner said accusingly.

"I didn't realize it till now."

"Can't have been missing it much, then."

"I guess she'll do," Sir Ludwig said over his shoulder to Mulliner. Another phrase to make the blood boil. Oh I must be better than a governess! I could not become accustomed to this manner of being put down.

"You're coming to Granhurst with me," Sir Ludwig said. "You have no objection, Miss—ah, Smith?" he asked, as he intercepted a flash of anger from me.

"I am in no position to object to anything. The house, I take it, is chaperoned? Your wife is there?"

"Really!" Mulliner exploded in a fine huff. "Upon my word, you must forgive her, Sir Ludwig."

"It is a reasonable question. You will be chaperoned," Sir Ludwig told me.

"You might take it as understood when *I* give my agreement to the proposal that there is nothing amiss in it," Mulliner chided me.

"Are we going now?" I asked the caller, enjoying the rudeness of ignoring Mulliner.

"Yes, it will save another trip to town tomorrow." Sir Ludwig took up his curled beaver from a table in the hall, and his gloves.

"I'll say goodbye to Miss Wickey then, and get my wrap." I whisked upstairs to do this.

Before saying goodbye to my one friend, I asked her for an assurance as to what sort of a gentleman Sir Ludwig might be. "He's all right. Don't be forward with him. Just do as he says and you'll rub along well enough. He'll be wanting you to look after his little sister, Abigail, I fancy. Not so little; she's fifteen, and a minx. Her governess got married last Halloween, and she's been without anyone to see to her lessons. The McCurdles told me he was looking about for a woman while he was in London, but he must have been out in his luck. In any case, it won't be for long, Miss Smith. Dr. Fell feels any day . . ."

"Yes, so he has been saying for ten days. Goodbye, Miss Wickey. I'll call when I'm in the village, if I can. I'll miss you." I gave her a hasty hug, thanked her as she stuffed one of her own little nightgowns and some lingerie into a bag, and I was off, carrying my sole earthly possessions on my back, and my borrowed ones in a brown paper bag that didn't weigh two pounds. This was traveling light!

Chapter Three

Sir Ludwig looked surprised when I handed my bag to him to carry. I had been surprised he hadn't reached out for it. In any case, he accepted it. "Is this all? You travel light," he said. Original! We took our leave of Mulliner and were out into the cold night, with the snow still on the ground. It reminded me of that other night, the night I had come to Wickey, except that it was not snowing now. There was a carriage and four horses waiting. Job horses, from the looks of them. They did not do justice to the smart carriage.

"My nags will be forwarded from Guildford," he said, as he caught me out examining the team. "I'm on my way home from London. I heard about your strange story at the inn where I stopped for dinner. In fact, I heard an intimation of it even as far away as Alton. Odd no one has come for you, when the tale is pretty broadly circulated. One assumes it has traveled in circles, and not only eastwards."

"Yes, the whole affair is very odd," I answered curtly,

and entered the door, to pull a fur rug over my knees and feel the welcome warmth of heated bricks.

"No idea at all how this might have come about?" he asked, in a spirit of civil conversation.

"None. I should not have stayed where I was if I had had a better place to go."

"You came to cuffs with Mulliner, I take it?"

"His housekeepr is very kind."

"Wickey's a darling. Did she tell you anything about me?"

"She said you have a sister who requires a governess. I doubt I'll prove a satisfactory one."

"I consider it a very temporary arrangement only. There isn't room at the rectory for a guest. Actually I had half decided to send Abbie to a ladies' seminary to put the final bit of polish on her before her coming out, but as you are so accomplished in French, you might make yourself useful in that area while you are with us."

"I shall be happy to," I answered, smothering down all my anger at 'making myself useful' to a set of rude country bumpkins.

"She will be happy to brush you up on your ciphering, a sphere in which I understand your own skills are lacking," he went on. "Abbie has a very German head on her shoulders. Keen on the sciences and mathematics. And she *looks* more German than myself, Miss Smith. My great-grandfather—as you appeared curious in my bearing a German name I mention it—was from Germany. He married an Englishwoman, however, and settled here a hundred or so years ago. All that remains of Germany is the name."

"I think something of the manner lingers," I disagreed politely. I don't know what he understood by the remark, but I meant to infer there was a Prussian abruptness and love of authority still in evidence.

"Quite possibly," he answered, unfazed.

We fell silent till we approached that area where I had been reborn, like Paul on the way to Damascus.

"This must be where it happened," I mentioned, to break the heavy silence.

He pulled down the window, hollered to his coachman, and the horses jingled to a halt. "Right here?" he asked.

"I believe that is the bunch of trees I remember going around in circles above me. There are none for some distance except these. This must be the spot."

"What, you were actually lying on the ground?"

"Yes, in that ditch over there."

He descended to view the place, and I too got out, unaided. "Were you hurt?"

"I had a bump on the head. I thought perhaps a branch hit me."

There was no sign of a large branch fallen, but it could have been picked up to use as firewood by a poor farmer. I had often seen them do it at home. I could even see the fustian jacket of a nameless phantom, on a nameless road somewhere in the foggy landscape of my past. Odd, useless bits of this sort surfaced regularly, but never anything of the least use. I mentioned the stage's passing at an appropriate hour, and the theory that I had asked to be put down from it.

"Why the devil would you do that? There's nothing within half a mile of here but Gwynne's place. Half a mile onwards, Theodore Gwynne's home. The name mean anything to you?"

"No, who is he?"

"A retired merchant from the city. A bachelor. We'll call on him and see if any bells ring. In fact, I want him to have a look at a painting I picked up at Sotheby's in London. It is called, optimistically I fear, a Vermeer. My father was used to do a spot of collecting. I usually pick up a clinker myself, but at the price this one was going for, I risked it."

"I should like to see it."

"You're interested in art?"

"Very much so, but not the Dutch genre school in particular."

"You remember all that, do you?" he asked, frowning.

"I remember irrelevant things."

"Who is to say they are irrelevant? You mentioned liking painting, missing your brushes you said as well. You alit here, and Gwynne is a fanatic on the subject of art. There must be some connection. We'll call on him tomorrow. Why, it begins to look as though we've solved your case already, Miss Smith. Odd no one thought of Gwynne living so close by."

"I was headed in the other direction. I mean—I decided to go that way. I don't actually know where I was on my way to."

"No one in Wickey seemed to know a thing about you, or to have been expecting you. You were likely headed to Gwynne's, all right. If you are known in artistic circles at all, Theo will know all about you. Come, we'll get back in the carriage. You have been ill."

On this occasion, Sir Ludwig held the door for me, rather impatiently to be sure, in a way that caused me to stop and look back down the road behind me, just to show him I was not impressed with his performance. "Remember something?" he asked.

"Yes, I am remembering how cold it was that night, almost like home."

"Home? The storm must have already started when you left your home, then. You can't be from very far away." But that wasn't the feeling I had. I seemed to recall cold winds blowing in from long ago and far away, blowing across hills, stony crops. Cornwall?

"We'll start investigating right away. Mulliner ought to have done it earlier," he said, taking my arm and propelling me into the carriage, still impatient.

I had again the sensation I didn't want any enquiries made, but I said nothing. Half a mile farther on, he pointed out the window. "That's Gwynne's place there. A little late to call on him tonight. He keeps early hours."

It was not later than nine, and the building was well

lit on the ground floor, giving the lie to this speech. I understood it to mean Sir Ludwig wished to get on home after a trip from London, and I was hardly in a mood for visiting myself. Another mile of silence and the carriage turned off the main road, up through a pair of stone pillars, along a quarter of a mile of snow-crusted pebbles, with a park around us, whose features were indistinguishable in the darkness. Only the welcome sight of lit windows was to be seen, looming suddenly ahead as we rounded a turn in the road. There was a fingernail of moon, enough to give a dim view of a large building of stone. It had a vaguely Classical feeling about it, with a few Corinthian columns to add to the illusion. It was only an illusion, the windows bore traces of Baroque, particularly in the second story where bulges of concrete protruded, yet it was too severely geometrical in other details to qualify as Baroque. A heavy-handed Germanic effort at elegance, I decided. The doorway in the distance had all the lack of joie de vivre to be expected of a *Schloss*. In my experience, the Germans do not excel in a doorway. They have mastered the window, even improved on it, but from old Schloss Langenburg to newish Schloss Fasanerie, one looks in vain for an exceptional doorway. The Italians have mastered it, and when they fail they at least throw up a row of columns to conceal the lack. The French hide it in the architecture, but do it with style. The English make a great thing of it, but the Germans give you a door that opens excellently without making one welcome. I never met a German yet who wouldn't give you an argument on the subject, and I was in no mood for an argument, so said nothing.

I stood regarding the house for some little time, with that old feeling coming over me, the feeling that I had been here before. Then a little laugh escaped me as I looked up and saw the clock in the central portion, embedded in the Mansard roof of the smaller top story, that did not extend to the building's edge. Schloss Ludwigsburg, of course! It was a sort of inferior copy of the famous home in Württemberg. "Are you related to *that* Ludwig?" I asked.

"No. My great-grandfather was an admirer of the German style, however, and had his architect copy a few features. My father in turn had the roof raised in emulation of the original. And *I* added the clock myself. What was it tipped you off? It is not that good a copy of the original."

"No, and the whole approach quite different. It must have been the clock. And of course the doorway," I added as we approached the entrance, a rounded arch, with the door recessed under it. It was a little finer than I expected at close range. Some effort at embellishment had been made, an ugly crest imbedded in concrete, with a rounded overhang above. Shabby actually, but the door opened well. Not a squeak or squawk. Inside we were not so opulent as our prototype. No moulded walls or ceilings, no cupids frolicking around miniature urns. Plain old English plaster and wood and paper, with the entrance floor courtesy of Connemara, Ireland. Furniture an eclectic blend accumulated over the generations, I assumed, by persons of very differing taste. Rather a pity to have a heavy Kent commode weighing some several hundred pounds as the focal point of the room, when there were more elegant and finer periods represented, but then arrival was early for rearranging Sir Ludwig's furnishings. It would come in time, no doubt, if I were fated to remain long at Granhurst. Certainly the elegant Chippendale gilt mirror gave the impression of a canary perched on an elephant's back, hung as it was too close above the Kent commode. As to hiding that long-case clock in a corner!

"We'll have tea," he said, interrupting my plans. I wanted a glass of decent wine and had hoped I might obtain one here, but then, with Sir Ludwig, I was fortunate he had not told me I would have a mug of beer. He left, to make a fresh toilette I supposed, certainly his mussed shirt collar stood in need of replacement. This gave me freedom to look around the Green Saloon. Hunter-green draperies—only a German would have such poor taste, and with no silk underhangings to lighten the oppression. The carpet had wine-colored roses on a salmon-pink ground, also not to my taste, but mercifully so well worn it need not distress the room much longer. The pictures on the walls goodish, but none of them my favorites. Stubbs and one grossly inferior Gainsborough. The latter gentleman ought not to have tackled animals. He made them look so very human, a sweet little girl kitten flirting with a boy spaniel. He should have stuck to his lovely lace trees and graceful ladies. The kitten lacked only a skirt and the rearrangement of ears to qualify for a lady.

I was standing back from the Gainsborough with these thoughts going through my head when I heard the whisper of a silken skirt at the door, and turned to find the raddled old face of a woman staring up at me, curiosity fairly leaping from blue eyes as sharp as a lynx's. She was very old, in her seventies at least, with wrinkles to which no one but Hogarth could have done justice. She belonged at the latter end of the Rake's Progress, this one. Soon Sir Ludwig lounged up behind her, making me realize how very tiny the lady was. Next to a midget. Also making me realize he had not taken time to change his shirt. No clothes-horses in the family, to judge by these two specimens.

"Cousin, allow me to present Miss Smith," he said, wearing a wary expression.

"Ah good, you've got a gel to put a rein on Abbie at last!" the dame shouted by way of welcome. "You'll never guess what the minx has been up to, Lud. Sneaked off into Wickey to get a look at that woman that lost her mind and is putting up with Mulliner. The creature was indisposed. They say she gives herself terrific airs."

"Actually it is her memory she lost, Cousin. Her temper too has the habit of going astray," he added, with a flicker of a dark eye towards me.

35

"Temper—ha, she has plenty of that I hear. They say she pulled little Tommy Green's ear nearly off his head for giving her some sauce."

"Before you regale us with more second-hand tales of goings-on at the rectory, let me make you known to Miss Smith. This is my late mother's cousin, Miss Smith. Miss Annie Enns. And Cousin, Miss Smith is the young lady who has been staying with Mulliner."

"You never mean you've brought her here!" Annie shouted. "We'll all be murdered in our beds." Then she turned to me. "Not to say I mean you will do it yourself, my dear, for no one has called you a murderess yet, but it is clear as a candle in the window someone was out to kill you. Can I see the bump on your head?"

"It has gone down," I told her, too astonished to show the degree of umbrage the occasion demanded. Never in all my life had I met anyone quite so outspoken as this.

"*All* down? What a pity. I would have liked very well to see it. But that is the way, good things never last a minute. If it had been a spot or freckles, it would hang on forever. Have you remembered who did it?" she asked with greedy interest.

"No, I don't think anyone tried to kill me. I fell, very likely."

"You don't look that gawky a creature to me, my dear. A great ladder of a girl to be sure, but you seem well formed and agile. Lud now, he was always so ungainly he couldn't cross a room without upsetting a chair."

I hadn't moved an inch since her entry, but then snap decisions were clearly her speciality. Ludwig saved the day. "Order us some tea, love," he commanded in his usual imperative style. There was no affection on the syllable 'love.'

She left, with a fearful glance over her shoulder at me, as though I meant to sneak up and give her a knock on the head. I felt like it. "Forgive her," Sir Ludwig said. "She meant no harm. Annie becomes very old."

"It is quite all right," I said in a failing voice, and walked to the sofa. Green plush—ugh!

"Odd, you know, that remark you made about Schloss Ludwigsburg. I have been thinking of that. Have you seen it?" he asked.

"Well, I think I have, but it may have been no more than a picture. Still, I seem to remember rain—standing in the rain looking at it. I don't know." These pictures, sometimes even moving pictures, darted into and out of my head so fast there was no pinning them down.

"Your speaking French so well and having been to Germany—it suggests a background of travel. Do you remember other places—foreign places?"

"Sometimes when I am in a warm room, I seem to think of olive trees, but I don't know what it may indicate." My eyes were always drawn to a picture; at this point I happened to glance at the Gainsborough.

"Do you know the artist of that?" he asked, jerking his head towards it.

"Of course. In fact, Gainsborough repeats himself. He uses that little dog in another picture—a portrait of a gentleman farmer sprawling over his gun. I don't recall the title, or where I saw it."

"You seem to know a good deal about art. Perhaps you'd like to look at my Vermeer while we await tea?"

"I am eager to see it."

It had been placed in the hallway, and was brought in now and unwrapped. What a disappointment! To think that Vermeer, that exquisite craftsman, had done this bad scene was ridiculous. It was from an earlier period, the drawing and design not nearly so well done as Vermeer's, the colors muddier. "Do you like it?" he asked.

"No. I dislike especially that it was sold to you as a Vermeer. Surely they wouldn't pull such a stunt on you at Sotheby's. It has an excellent reputation."

"It wasn't exactly sold as a Vermeer, though the name certainly arose. I paid very little for it."

"One can pick up a real Vermeer cheaply. He is

underestimated at the moment. Not popular at all. What did you pay?"

"A little under a hundred pounds."

"If you like it, it will not go amiss in some quiet corner of a study."

"What makes you so sure it isn't a Vermeer?"

"He would never paint anything so unbalanced. His paintings are models of proportion, composition. The window there on the right with the sun streaming through needs some counterbalance on the other side. It has none. You may rest assured Vermeer would have provided you a bright balance on the other side, a white blouse, a brass pot, or a mirror picking up the sunshine. And he would have rendered the sunshine more realistically, too."

He pushed the painting aside, just as Miss Annie entered in front of a servant carrying a tea tray. "Bought another picture, have you, Lud?" she asked with interest. "What have we got this time? Bah, another homely Dutch woman holding a jug. I hope you don't mean to stick her in my room. Here, I've brought you a nice cup of tea, Miss Smith. Do you remember what tea is? It's for drinking, in these things we call cups." She lifted a cup and held it up to me for viewing and recalling.

"Thank you," I said in a very weak voice.

"Ho, you'll catch back on to things in no time." Then she added in a perfectly audible aside to Sir Ludwig, "I daresay it is all a hum she pulled the little McKay boy's ear off. She seems as sane as you or me." Then she turned back to me, smiling away. "Well, Miss Smith, I'll give you lessons myself and teach you all sorts of things. I'm sorry I was rude to you before. It will be great fun, having a looney with us. We are very dull here. Lud never has a word to say for himself from week's end to week's end."

This pleasant remark nudged him into speech. "Has Abbie gone to bed?" he asked, to divert her stream of insults.

"Yes, she's biting her nails again. I gave her a good

spanking and sent her to bed. She ain't talking to me, thank God. She'll be glad to see you, Miss Smith. When did you remember your name, eh?"

"I didn't. Mr. Mulliner decided on the name."

"Ah, he would, the old stick. Smith—what a lack of imagination. I shall call you Miss Trelawney. Isn't that a grand name? I have been wishing I knew someone to call Miss Trelawney. It breathes of romance, and you are romantical, having such a history. Rose Trelawney we'll call her, eh Lud?"

"That is up to Miss Smith," he said, and with a weary sigh he reached out to pour his own tea, as his cousin made no move to do so, and I was seated well away from the tray.

"What has *she* got to say about it? We may call her what we wish. Besides, she won't know the difference, poor thing."

After he had poured three cups, without a single word of reply to his cousin's speech, but only a harried glance at her, I arose and handed one cup to Miss Annie.

"She has *some* manners, you see. She is not a complete savage as the McCurdles are saying," she informed him. "Cream and five spoons of sugar, Rose," she commanded me sternly. I added these revolting supplies and gave the cup back to her, taking up a cup for myself, with cream only. "You want sugar in that," she told me. "We ain't poor. I daresay Mulliner didn't put any sugar on the table, the skint. He is our cousin, you must know. Lud gave him the living at Wickey to get him off our backs. He only gets two hundred and fifty a year."

"He is a connection merely," Sir Ludwig corrected hastily. A very distant connection surely, or Mr. Mulliner would have been prating of it.

I settled back with my tea, still without sugar. I had fallen into this habit at Mulliner's, not so much to save his sugar as to slim down my figure. I sat waiting to hear what outrage the old dame would say next.

"The dog peed on the carpet in your room," she informed her cousin. "That demmed pregnant spaniel it was."

"Too bad. I trust it was cleaned up," he replied in a tone that held much of mortification in it.

"I gave her a good kick you may be sure. Had her tied up in the barn and took a stick to her."

"I won't have my dogs beaten!" he shouted angrily.

"No, only your family!"

I looked with a little upsurge of fear towards my host, but the line of defeat of his shoulders soon removed the fear, and even incited me to a shred of pity. "He beats his sister," Miss Annie announced triumphantly. "He'll beat you, too, if you don't do as he says. All the child did was to take a run on his hunter, and he . . ."

"Annie, if you please!" he said in a loud, grim voice. "Miss Smith is not interested in our domestic squabbles."

"Beat her and sent her to her room to *starve*!" She drew out the last word in a horrible manner, the eyes sparkling with pleasure. She was as mad as a Bedlamite.

"Gave her one swat across the bottom, and made her go without dinner. My hunters can be dangerous to an inexperienced rider," Sir Ludwig explained to me in a strained voice.

"Ha, but I fooled him. Took her up a nice piece of plum cake."

"You couldn't have made it meat and potatoes!" he expostulated. "Stuffing the girl with sweets. She'll turn into a dumpy, fat Fräulein." He went on with a few more angry remarks. Remembering the origin of the word 'German', from the Celtic meaning 'shout', I smiled at the appropriateness of it. It was no quiet, civilized household I had chanced into. Between the three of them, it seemed things would be lively.

"Abbie is skin and bones, like Miss Rose Trelawney," Annie said, with a disparaging look, not at me, but my sugarless cup. "Well now," she ran on, "so Miss

Trelawney is to be Abbie's governess, is she? Do you know anything about the job?"

"I had a governess myself. I have some idea how to proceed," I told her.

"How do you know you did?" she asked craftily. "I thought you couldn't remember things."

"I don't *know* exactly . . . that is . . . I must have." I fell into a little quandary at the question. No helpful image of one specific governess arose to aid me.

"Don't pester Miss Smith, Annie," Ludwig said.

"How is she going to remember things if we don't ask her questions? Ha, I've got it!" she declared in a bright voice. "We'll give her a tap on the head. That's how she lost her mind, and that's how we'll bring it back. Don't stare, Lud. It works, I tell you. Your cousin, that muffin-faced girl they was trying to get you to marry, she took a spill from her horse, a clumsy woman she was, so bow-legged her skirts stuck out with it, and didn't know her name for three hours. Then a glass of water fell off the shelf onto her head, and it all came back." She eyed the teapot as she spoke, finding boiling hot tea a suitable replacement for a glass of water, no doubt.

"May I be shown to my room?" I asked, suddenly overcome by so much nonsense.

"Where are you putting her?" Annie asked.

"The blue room, next Abbie."

"It's haunted," she told me with a happy smile. Quite a treat! "Lud's great-grandfather murdered his sweetheart in that room. She was his wife's half sister, and she comes back to haunt people. Adeline is her name. I like her excessively. Come, I'll introduce you."

"I'll show Miss Smith up," Sir Ludwig said, arising with a resigned look.

I took up my brown paper bag and followed him from the room, after making a curtsey to his crazy cousin. "Goodnight, Rose Trelawney," she called happily. When I left, she was merrily spooning a pound of sugar into an inch of tea, and humming to herself. I wondered who was my chaperone, a Bedlamite in her seventies, or a young lady of fifteen years.

"My cousin is not usually so—strange," he said, in the spirit of an apology as we went up the stairs. "I hope you will not be troubled by either ghosts or fears of a beating. If she has taken a stick to my dogs I may have to have her restrained. But really, she is quite harmless, in the general way."

I nodded in understanding of his predicament. He opened a door into a pretentious chamber, hung in deep, dusty shades of blue, with a canopied bed that reached nearly to the ceiling. "That contraption is for sleeping in, I presume? A bed it is called, is it not? It all comes back to me now."

"Annie was correct about one thing. Smith is too bland a name for you." He pointed to the walls. "Plenty of pictures there for you to disparage and find a fault with before you go to sleep. I believe you mentioned recalling the matter of sleep." He turned to make an exit then turned back with a doubtful look on his face. Its cause was soon apparent. He was trying to figure out my position in his household. "Shall I send a girl to you?" he asked, uncertain.

"No thank you. I can take Kitty's nightdress out of the bag myself. Goodnight, Sir Ludwig."

"Sleep well, Miss Trelawney." He bowed and the door was opened wider. Then he turned back as he went out to say, "Wickey is the lady's name. Miss Wickey."

"Oh yes, so it is."

Kitty—how odd I should twice call Miss Wickey by that absurd name. She was more mouse than kitten.

Chapter Four

I dreamed that night of Scotland. One of the pictures on the wall which Sir Ludwig mistakenly put in the darkest corner was a rather fine etching of a medieval Scottish castle, its turrets resting on heavy moulding, stretching into a cloud-scudded sky. I looked to the etching to see how accurately I had dreamed, and was surprised to see the picture differed considerably from my dream. It was not Castle Fraser at all, as I had thought. Odd, but the picture had triggered the dream no doubt. I had been walking over highlands, smelling heather and seeing many sheep. One had the raddled face of Miss Annie, another no face at all, but only a smooth blank where a face should be. It was of the most interest to me. It seemed absolutely vital that I put a face on that unknown sheep. The dream was still with me, vividly, along with a sharp sense of urgency. Something to do with my past, obviously. Someone I wanted to remember? But why had I put that someone in the form of a sheep? And what was a smooth black kitten doing amidst the herd of sheep? It should have been a sheepdog. I felt almost on the edge of knowledge. As if, once I got the answer to these few questions, I should know everything. Then the feeling fell away quickly as I glanced around the strange room. The memory of where I was and what awaited me overcame all these vague tatters of thoughts, and I sat up quickly.

In a minute I had washed and outfitted myself in the omnipresent blue bombazine. How I wished for a new gown! And shoes to fit. These were an inconvenient half inch too long. Was someone, somewhere, wearing a pair half an inch too short? She must be even more uncomfortable than myself. It was still early when I went belowstairs, only eight-thirty, but the Kessler ménage was already assembled at table, tucking into a large repast. Sir Ludwig presented me to his sister, a sprightly young lady in her early teens, with brown hair and blue eyes. The 'skin and bones' Annie had referred to were accompanied by approximately one hundred and forty pounds of firm flesh. Another ten pounds and she would indeed be a fat Fräulein. The breakfast on her plate indicated she would add five of the ten before noon. But she was pretty, also full of curiosity. No doubt Miss Annie had given her a rundown on me. I assumed, when her greeting was proper to the point of blandness, that her brother as well had had a few words with her. She was 'very pleased to make my acquaintance' and 'hoped I would be comfortable at Granhurst.' Other than staring at me with all her might, she did nothing outrageous over breakfast. Miss Annie made minute enquiries for Adeline. I told her she was fine.

"Ah good! She has got over her cold, then," Miss Annie said nonchalantly, and spooned gobs of marmalade on to her plate. How did she keep her wizened little figure? She ought to be rolling in balls of fat. The whole family ate ravenously. They needed a firm hand on their diets, and would soon have one. "Lud tells me he is taking you to see Gwynne this morning."

"What about my lessons?" Miss Kessler asked. I doubted it was an eagerness to get at her French that instigated the question. She wanted to examine the looney more closely.

"Your sudden bout of eagerness will have to wait till after lunch," her brother told her, undeceived.

The only real unpleasantness over the repast was Miss Annie's asking, "Rose is going to eat with us, like a guest, is she?" I assumed the last governess had not done so. Perhaps I ought not to have come into the family parlor. I must say no other course so much as occurred to me. If I had been a governess in my last incarnation, I had been treated as family.

I looked up with a guilty start at the question, feeling suddenly very ill at ease. "Miss Smith *is* a guest, who has kindly offered to teach Abbie a little French," Sir Ludwig said in a damping way.

"Said she was a governess," Annie contradicted.

Abigail opened her mouth to second this speech, but she was silenced by a blighting stare from her brother, who rapidly spoke up to request more coffee, if it was not too much trouble.

"Are you paying her then?" was Annie's next speech.

It threw him for a total loss. I think the matter had not occurred to him. It had to me. I was very eager to get my hands on some cash, to augment my infinitesimally small wardrobe. "We haven't discussed that," he replied.

He left very soon afterwards, but his authority remained behind him, preventing the ladies from pestering me. Soon I too arose to don my cape and go out to the carriage. We used only a pair for the short trip to Gwynne's, a good team, therefore Sir Ludwig's own, I supposed.

Mr. Gwynne's home was of red brick, large and square and modern, with very little adornment on the exterior. It was the reverse of Granhurst, all opulence within, painted ceilings, chandeliers, touches of gilt

45

everywhere, in overly ornate poor taste. *Nouveau riche* run riot. Mr. Gwynne, however, appeared a sensible man. His first interest was not the local freak—he did no more than nod and smile when Sir Ludwig mentioned who I was—but the *soi-disant* Vermeer, which had been brought along for showing.

"Let's have a look at her," Gwynne said eagerly, rubbing his hands in anticipation, then snatching the package from Kessler's fingers, unable to contain his eagerness. "Ah, too bad," he said, shaking his head after no more than a glance at the thing. "The Guild of St. Luke, right enough, but not Vermeer," he told the owner.

Dutch painting was not so well known to me that I could second this opinion regarding the guild, but I was happy to hear confirmed my view that the work was not an authentic Vermeer, and for the reasons I had mentioned. Sir Ludwig's eyes were more often on myself than the picture during this discussion. At its termination, he told Mr. Gwynne our thoughts, that I had been on my way to see him when I had suffered my accident, and asked if he had been expecting a young lady.

"No, I wasn't," he said, astonished at the idea. "I have never seen Miss Smith before in my life. I was expecting no one."

"The lady's name is not actually Smith. We feel she has had some doings in the world of art, and hoped you might provide us a lead as to who she might be," Sir Ludwig continued.

"I have correspondence with many people, including some ladies, both here in England and abroad, on the subject of acquiring paintings for my collection, but beyond that, I can tell you nothing," he said.

Kessler pressed on to request the names of some of these ladies, but we both knew I was no Italian contessa, nor Austrian princess, certainly not Lady Melbourne. It was pointless. We had drawn a blank here. Mr. Gwynne was always eager to meet a fellow connoisseur, however, and wasn't about to let us away that easily. We were led into a long picture gallery, whose walls were hung with a miscellany of paintings. There was everything from early Renaissance works, even one slant-eyed Madonna going back to the Byzantine period, to recent portraits by Lawrence and Reynolds. He was no specialist as to period—he bought what pleased him, he said. We admired the works together, we three, never really agreeing on anything. Sir Ludwig had a taste for voluptuous, writhing naked women by Rubens; Gwynne some leaning towards the French Directory period. The former was too emotional for me, the latter lacking in emotion. I confess I prefer a dainty, pretty picture. Fragonard, Watteau—elegant trifles. Gainsborough sans animals pleases me as well as any English painter. Gwynne was soon patronizing me, and before I became sharp with him, I began patronizing Kessler, in which pursuit Gwynne was not slow to second me. Sir Ludwig did not come right out and say he didn't know much about art, but he knew what he liked, but he did admit he was less informed on the matter than his father, who had apparently been a bit of a dab, and an old friend of Gwynne's. "But if art is supposed to represent beauty, then I'll pick Rubens," he finished up, with a last lecherous look at a plump blond lady, who was being hauled under a tree by a satyr.

I nearly missed the most interesting piece in the gallery. It was not hanging on the wall, being an oddly-shaped piece painted on wood, with hinges on its left side. It went up to a point on the right side and was straight along the other edges. Half a pointed doorway it was, one third of a triptych. The large central portion was missing, as was the right-hand hinged piece. Assembled in toto, the work would make up a central panel, with pieces half the size to close over in front showing one picture, to be opened to reveal the large panel beneath. He had his fraction mounted on a fancy tripod. It was a madonna, undoubtedly the work of the fifteenth century Italian sometime monk, Fra Filippo Lippi. Yes, no one but that rogue would paint such a saucy, pert madonna—some urchin from the streets he was making up to whom he had used for his model. One half expected her to look up and wink, despite her halo. "The Missing Madonna!" I exclaimed, lifting it up to carry it to a window for closer examination.

"Ah, you are familiar with the Medici triptych!" Mr. Gwynne said in approving accents. "It is not well known, Miss Smith. You have indeed a good eye to recognize it."

"Oh, was it painted for a Medici? Cosimo, I daresay. I had thought it must be from a church."

"The family chapel," he corrected happily. "I picked it up for a song at a little street auction in London. I would love to get ahold of the other two pieces. Traced the owner, but he knew nothing of the thing's history. He bought it in Italy a few years ago, just the one piece, as an oddity, but found it didn't hang well. It would hang well if I could get the rest of it. I wish I could do it."

"I wish I could!" I heard myself say.

"Aye, it would be something to reassemble it. We haven't much from such an early period of Italian art here in England. This predates Botticelli, daVinci and so on," he continued to Kessler. "Mid-fifteenth century, the *quattrocento*. The central portion is thought to be the Christ child with angels, and the right door St. Joseph. A nativity scene it was, I believe. I came across a description of such a work in any case, and believe this is what I have a piece of. How did you come to know of it, Miss Smith?"

I shook my head. "I've never seen this before. I recognized Fra Lippi's style from a convent in Florence."

"Ah, you have been to Italy," Mr. Gwynne said, looking at me with interest.

"Oh yes, I liked Italy best of all till . . ." Realizing Sir Ludwig was staring at me open-mouthed, I stopped to think what I was saying. I had been to Italy then, and other places. Unless I lied; unless I dreamed it in those strangely vivid dreams I had. And why had I stopped liking Italy best of all? I felt suddenly very warm, could almost smell the hot dust blowing through the olive trees.

Mr. Gwynne would have liked to discuss Italy, but realized from my sudden silence and Ludwig's stare that I was distressed. "Let us have a cup of tea," he said kindly. We left the gallery and went into the tasteless saloon for tea. Odd that with all his love of beauty and apparent wealth Mr. Gwynne could not have contrived a more pleasing saloon for himself. It was garishly red and blue, with plush and velvet everywhere.

"Strange your eye picking out my madonna," Gwynne rattled on. "Not the most valuable piece in that room, not the prettiest, but the most curious I think. I mentioned I am trying to get the rest of it. Mr. Uxbridge over in Shaftesbury is said to have a line on something from the *quattrocento*. Painted on wood. I am in touch with him in writing. I was to go to him when that dreadful storm came up. Wouldn't it be something if it were the large central panel! Then I would lack only the other door."

I could hardly listen to his chatter. I kept seeing that saucy madonna, smiling at me in a knowing way surely never used by any madonna. It excited me strangely, touched off some responsive chord in that muddled mind of mine. I wanted to get away and think. I was little enough addition to the polite tea table chatter. We soon left, with Mr. Gwynne urging us to return, promising to show us more treasures, scattered about in rooms abovestairs.

"So you've been to Italy as well as Germany," Sir Ludwig said as we went down to the carriage. "I hope you hadn't come directly from one of those foreign shores before you fell off that stage, or we'll never find out who you are."

"I'm not sure about Germany."

"It don't rain in *libraries*, where people look at pictures of houses, Miss Smith. What is it about this madonna has you excited? Is it the thing's age?"

"No. No, it's not that."

"Is it very valuable?"

"If it were all put together . . . but it's not that. It's more the mystery of it. The fact of its being broken up and the pieces scattered." But of course it wasn't that, either.

"What interests *me* is how our friend Lippi convinced a knowing gent like Cosimo he was painting anything other than a trollop. It must be a sacrilege to give a madonna so much the appearance of a baggage."

"Cosimo was strangely tolerant of Fra Lippi's pranks. He stopped locking him in his studio when he sneaked out the window on a sheet. But he was ill employed to do sacred paintings."

He shook his head as we entered the carriage. "I feel it bizarre you remember such obscure facts, and can't recall your own name. We'll put notices in the papers, giving a description of you and where you are to be located."

"No!"

"Why not?" he asked, blinking.

I felt deeply troubled, agitated to the marrow of my bones. "Not yet," I prevaricated.

"My dear girl, if you come from some far distant corner of the kingdom such as Cornwall or Scotland, we will *never* learn who you are. It must be done. Too much time has been wasted already."

"It can't do any harm to wait a few more days. Let me think—try to remember. Please!" There was a wildly desperate note in my voice. I heard it with wonder, and so, I fear, did Sir Ludwig. I couldn't help it. I was afraid.

"Have you been telling me the truth?" he asked baldly. "Are you in some sort of trouble? Have you done something foolish—stolen something?" His hands gestured vaguely to denote his inability to categorize my crime.

"No! I don't think so. It's not like that. It's worse than that."

"Good God, you haven't *killed* someone!" he shouted.

"Don't be absurd." But I felt a moisture spring out on my forehead and between my shoulderblades here in the cool carriage. I nearly fainted for the awful feeling of doom that came over me. I felt weak, trembling. Was it only Fell's 'fear of the unknown' that distressed me so?

Sir Ludwig said no more on the matter, but tucked the blanket around me to stop my shivering. "I had planned to go on into the village and pick up some newspapers. It would save having the horses put to again. You have no objection? There might be some mention of you."

"Please do it," I said, recovering rapidly at this indication he would not blazon my story across the news sheets.

"If you remember anything, anything at all, tell me. I cannot believe you have run seriously afoul of the law. Darting away from home for one reason or another is more like it. I want you to promise you will tell me."

"I will."

I don't know what he could have been thinking. My reactions certainly indicated guilt. "We'll speak of other things," he went on. "This distresses you too much. You will be wanting to pick up a few personal items in Wickey I imagine. Why don't you do that while I arrange to have newspapers sent to me?"

"I do need things, but I have no money."

"You can repay me when you discover your family, if it will make you feel better."

"What if I never do?"

"Then you will have a long time to work off the debt," he pointed out reasonably, refusing to comfort me with sympathy. I had never found the German people to be overly encumbered with sympathy. Their loud voices might give rise to the notion they are emotional, but the voice is more likely to be raised in anger, or even cheer. Not sympathy.

"Your sister will not require a governess for the rest of her life," I returned, taking up his practical tone.

"By the time Abbie is popped off, Annie will need a keeper. You must allow me to apologize for her. She was a dear when she was more herself, younger. She still is at times, but she becomes senile, or mischievous. I'm not at all sure she couldn't keep herself under better control if she wanted. It must be wonderful to be able to blurt out whatever is in your head, and know you will be excused for it, however outrageous."

I had not observed Sir Ludwig to use much restraint on his tongue, but I didn't feel like an argument. "Does she really believe in ghosts?"

"Only since she discovered it irks me."

We were driving past my Damascus again, and again I looked at the place helplessly. "You wouldn't—you couldn't possibly have been coming to see *me* that night you got down from the stage?" he asked, frowning. "I am a mile farther away than Gwynn, and as you were not going *there*—is it possible you were en route to Granhurst? The house seemed familiar to you . . ."

"I don't think so. Were you expecting someone?"

"No. When you run out of sane ideas you start coming up with nonsensical ones. Now what was a well-traveled lady with a good knowledge of art doing on the stage to Winchester—or possibly on to London. More peculiarly, why did she get off that stage, in the middle of a storm?" We sat in silence for a long minute. "I wonder if you weren't going *to* anywhere in particular, but getting off the stage because of some danger there. Maybe you recognized someone on it—or took the notion that whoever was going to meet you represented danger . . ." He looked for signs of acceptance of these theories.

I regarded him disconsolately. "Well, dammit, there must have been *some* reason!" he shouted, turning

German on me again. "The only thing that has interested you in the least is that painted door. Is it possible you were going to see it?"

This I could credit. I had strong feelings about it, but the facts didn't bear me out. "Gwynne says not."

"We should have asked him if he was in contact with any lady about it. We didn't ask him that specifically. I'll go back later, or send him a note."

We reached the village and had the carriage stabled at the inn. It was my first public foray into Wickey. I had met several of the inhabitants at the rectory, but never gone out. Knowing I was a subject of lively gossip, I was reluctant to venture into the shops. Some of these feelings must have been evident on my face. "Do you want me to go with you?" he asked.

"No, thank you." His presence while I purchased undergarments and personal articles would be no better than facing the hordes of Wickey alone.

"I'll tell them at the drapery shop you are with me, and are to use my account, to preclude any unpleasantness on that score," he mentioned. Harper's was called a drapery shop, but had expanded over the years to include a great diversity of articles. It was the only large shop in Wickey, actually.

Sir Ludwig was greeted by a servile clerk, fawning on him and doing everything but licking his boots. He was a good spender, then. The clerk prepared to attach himself to my elbow once our business was explained. Kessler got rid of him very effectively. "That will be all, thank you," he said, and turned away from the man to give me instructions. "Don't feel obliged to restrict yourself to navy bombazine, Miss Smith. Buy something to do justice to your silken petticoats, and your Continental travels." He left before I could fashion a setdown to this piece of impertinence. Knew very well he had been bold too, to judge from the haste with which he removed himself from my tongue.

The shop held only one other customer, a woman not known to me, though she suspected my identity. When

I saw her whispering in the corner with the clerk I made sure her suspicions were being confirmed. But as she contented herself to spy on me from an aisle away, I ignored her. I also took my host's advice. I bought a dainty pair of patent slippers that fit beautifully. I was surprised to find such a good quality in Wickey. I also bought the necessary items of undergarments and a bolt of pretty green shotsilk, with gold for piping and buttons. Reckless with Kessler's credit, I helped myself to a nice paisley fringed shawl to pretty up my navy bombazine till the green should be made up, and got some tortoiseshell combs and ribbons of various colors for my hair. The cosmetics counter lured me into other purchases—a bottle of Denmark lotion, a new soap from Austria that had to be whipped up like cream before it was applied, a box of powder, a bottle of scent. Not the average purchases of a governess, but surely required to match my petticoats. Imagine, my *petticoats* were a subject of local gossip! How Ivor would hate it, I thought with a smile, then came abruptly up against this new name. Who was *Ivor* that he should care my petticoats were discussed? No face, no relationship followed the name. A father, brother, beau, husband? No—I wore no wedding ring. Fiancé, perhaps? A fiancé would feel a proprietary interest in his bride's petticoats.

Sir Ludwig was back in three-quarters of an hour, before I had half finished looking around, with a load of newspapers in his arms, and the word that he had left an order for future issues at the office of the stage. "All set?" he asked briskly.

I had some thoughts of picking up a pair of galoshes, new gloves and several other trifles, but a glance to the mound of items to be presented to him, sitting on the counter already wrapped and a bill beside them, caused me to reconsider. "All set," I answered. "Those few things there." His eyes widened at the sight, and I thought it a good time to rush on with my single piece of memory, to distract him.

"Oh by the way, I have remembered something," I said, piling his arms high.

"I can't carry any more. We'll have to come back," he said, impatiently.

"No, it's not that! I remember Ivor."

"Ivor who?" he asked with interest. The trick worked nicely. He hardly glanced at the bill before nodding at it and saying to the clerk it was fine.

"Well I haven't remembered his *last* name yet." I dashed ahead to hold the door open. "But when I thought of everyone talking about my petticoats, it suddenly struck me that Ivor would not like it. He must be someone close to me. A fiancé, I thought he might be."

"Maybe a brother."

"Possibly, but would a brother care about that?"

"I would dislike to have Abigail's petticoats discussed in quite the public way yours have been."

"Isn't it horrid? A person has absolutely no privacy when she is in such a position as I am. I daresay the whole village will know before nightfall that I bought two ells of green silk, and a bottle of Denmark Lotion."

"Several other items as well," he pointed out, shifting the load. I took some newspapers that were slipping from beneath the bags.

"I—I had no hairbrush, you see, only a comb Miss Wickey lent me, and my shoes were too big, and one can't hobble along on *one* pair of stockings or—or other things that have to be washed so often."

"Very true. The town will now have the satisfaction of knowing what goes under the petticoats, and what you wear to bed."

"You'd think people would have better things to do than gossip so."

"The cats haven't been so happy in an age. The McCurdles will be in despair to have missed your shopping spree. I fancy Miss Gretch is on her way there now to report. She was in the shop I noticed."

"Odious people will always talk and make a to-do

over nothing. It is always like that." My companion discerned no importance in the speech, but I suddenly knew this was not the first time I had been gossiped about. I was used to it, in fact. I had been held up as a bad example before. I was becoming immensely interested in myself, quite as a separate entity from Miss Smith.

"Let's get home. I'm starved," Sir Ludwig said prosaically.

"After that *huge* breakfast?" I asked, with more than polite surprise in my voice. It was time to begin the family's diet.

"I don't call that a huge breakfast—only gammon and three eggs."

"And *four* muffins! But then you are a large man," I added, hoping to imply he was larger than was pleasing. He was not fat to be sure, but there was a certain bulkiness that could be trimmed to advantage. I always preferred lithe, elegant gentlemen.

"Thank you," he answered, mistaking it for a compliment! It was a little early in our acquaintance to disillusion him, and a poor time too, with his arms holding my shopping. "You ought to eat a little more," he suggested, with a speculative glance over the parcels at my cape, which was all concealing. If he had a memory at all, he knew what was beneath it. He had looked hard enough the night before at the rectory. "You are a little thin."

"I was considering going on a diet," I answered, astonished.

"The proper diet will build you up. You don't require more than ten pounds to be the right size."

I was too nonplussed to reply, but with a memory of his preferred painting, the bulging Rubens lady, I think he had a poor notion of what ten pounds would do to my figure. Fifty was more like it!

Chapter Five

When we sat down to luncheon, it was clear Cousin Annie was also starved, and bent on satisfying her hunger with nothing but bread and sweets. It was quite simply frightening to watch her make a meal of bread and honey, while meat and cheese sat on the table, untasted. As she was on the downward path to senility, I did not feel she required all the tact and respect accorded to the normally aged. I judiciously slipped the honey beyond her reach; when she asked for it, I passed along the cheese instead, as though by error.

She smiled at me indulgently. "That is *cheese*, Rose," she told me. "I want honey."

"So much of it is not good for you," I told her, and continued pressing forward the cheese.

She first shot an angry glance at me from those bright blue eyes, but I smiled blandly, and then a crafty look came over her face. "If you say so, Rose," she said, and took a slice of cheese. She informed

Abigail in a loud aside, "We must humor her, poor thing, till she gets her mind back."

With this idea in my pocket, I quite insisted she try a slice of the mutton. In this, too, she humored me, as I humored her by calling it bacon, which sent her off into trills of delighted laughter. "Have some *bacon*, Lud," she said, passing the mutton along to him with a broad wink.

"Sir Ludwig has already had bacon," I told her, with a look to his plate, where a thick slice still sat. Encouraging him to eat more was a mile from my mind. But he had not tumbled to my hint, and took another slice, which I could not well prevent.

I concentrated on Annie during that meal, with good success. Under my eye, Abbie too was eating heavily, but till I got to know her a little, I would wait. Kessler regarded me closely, first with surprise at my gall, but as he realized it was working so well, the surprise turned to tolerant amusement. At the meal's conclusion he said to me, "If you call the French lesson German you will induce my sister to partake of it as painlessly as Annie the mutton."

As it turned out, it was less painful than that. Of course it wasn't much of a lesson. At no time was it *la plume de ma soeur sur le bureau de mon frère*. Nor did we get right down to nasty irregular verbs and subjunctives, but conversed in French, with myself correcting her pronunciation and vocabulary, also her ideas, upon occasion, though to be sure this had nothing to do with French. Had she ever been exposed to French haute couture, however, she would not have expressed such a lively appreciation for a ghastly cerise gown with black ribbons. We had our lesson over my purchases and her fashion magazines. And why not? A lady is as likely to be discussing fashions as any more serious matter in either French or English.

The precise matter under discussion was a pattern to go with my green shot silk. Abbie's selection of a gown with a plunging neckline and no sleeves was a trifle risqué for a sometime governess. I chose, instead, a modest model that I fully intended garnishing with all manner of lace and ribbons. It was an afternoon gown, fitted, with long sleeves. I had no pattern of any kind, but allowed myself, in my eagerness to get on with it, to be convinced none was necessary. Abbie measured me, thus providing an excellent chance to review our numbers in French, along with various parts of the anatomy. I also expressed, in English to be sure she didn't miss the point, horror at the largeness of my dimensions, which were a good several inches smaller than her own. I expostulated on the impossibility of appearing elegant with a full figure.

"Lud likes a well-rounded figure," she told me. "He thinks I am just right, and he used to call me scarecrow when I was thinner."

A bit tricky convincing her her brother was old-fashioned, but a conscientious pointing out of the slender models in the magazines who looked so well in the gowns made her bite her lip in indecision. "*I* mean to shed five pounds in any case," I concluded.

"Maybe I should, too," she decided. It was a start.

I wondered during the afternoon how Annie was amusing herself. Abigail, with whom I nearly instantly achieved a first-name basis, told me it was her custom to either sleep or talk to Adeline. Talking to Adeline indicated she was prowling in my room, but with my precious purchases still in bags before me on the table, there was little enough mischief she could do there. I didn't give a thought to Sir Ludwig. A man would have his own business to attend to, but when he entered the parlor where we worked some hours later, it turned out he had devoted himself to my problem. He was carrying the armful of papers purchased in Wickey.

"I don't see anything about you in here," he said, dumping them on top of my green silk. "Maybe you'd like to have a look later."

With a little grimace of annoyance I removed them from my new material, looking for inkstains on it.

Abigail, more at ease with him, castigated him as 'the rudest brother in captivity,' which had not the least effect, though he said 'Sorry,' in a perfunctory way.

"Gwynne had no news about the Italian madonna, either. I sent over a note and had my boy wait for an answer. He was in touch with no one but this fellow over Shaftesbury way about it. It looks as though we've reached a dead end. Nothing to do now but wait for the other papers to arrive."

"You will be regretting your haste in having me here, as it seems the visit is to be a prolonged one."

"Not at all. We enjoy the novelty of having a looney amongst us," he answered in a perfectly civil tone.

"Ludwig!" Abbie gasped, looking to me for signs of offense.

"You have no idea how very much at home you manage to make me feel. But our collective wits are gone begging—only to be expected of course, mad as we all are. It is Bedlam we ought to have been in touch with! No doubt I escaped from there."

"Or Bridewell," he suggested, still politely.

"The women's prison is a distinct possibility, except that I came from the wrong direction. I was not escaping from London."

"We don't know that you were escaping from anywhere. We do suspect, however, that you came from the direction of Shaftesbury—where that Uxbridge fellow interested in the madonna comes from. Gwynne is in touch with him. I'll ask him to mention you, if you have no objection?"

"None in the world."

Sir Ludwig was casting an eye on the pattern book by this time, mentally selecting the model he would prefer I suppose. "This is a nice one," he said, pointing out the same vulgar cerise gown chosen by his sister.

I could only stare. Such poor taste was not unusual in a young girl of unformed ideas, but a fully grown man ought to have known better. "I doubt it is the style worn by your last governess," I mentioned.

"Very true," he said nodding, and still looking at the book, with an occasional flicker of the eyes towards myself. "But our last governess was not such a prodigiously handsome creature. I am indebted to Annie for the delightful description. I am not poetical myself."

"I am indebted to you for the advice on the gown, but shall seek my own counsel *quand même*."

"I begin to see that is your usual way of going on. Your speaking a word of French reminds me I interrupt the French lesson," he said, with a pointed look at the fashion books and material. Then he strolled from the room.

"He likes you," Abbie said with an impish smile. It was difficult to imagine from whence she pulled this notion. "You know how to handle him," she expanded. "My last governess used to go into a quake and think she was about to be fired when he tried to roast her."

"He may fire me if he wishes, but he will lose out on the ten guineas I owe him if he does."

Sir Ludwig showed not the least intention of dispensing with my somewhat erratic services over the next few days. I was shockingly tiresome, and expensive too. Quite ruined the green shot silk by cutting it out without a pattern, thus making the waist too small, for we didn't leave enough width for the seams. Annie snapped the ruined material up. Being not an inch over four feet eleven, she felt there was enough good cloth left in the skirt to make her an outfit. It was never done, but she liked the color, and often wrapped it around her shoulders on a chilly afternoon or evening. Abigail and I made another trip into Wickey to buy new material and hire a dressmaker. We also stopped to visit Miss Wickey and return her borrowed garments. When she enquired how my green silk gown turned out, and why I wasn't wearing it, I knew my shopping trip with Sir Ludwig was public knowledge.

For the second new gown I selected a perfectly hideous bordeaux color. I don't know what made me do it, except that Abbie insisted it was lovely. The other expense was Sir Ludwig's own fault. He often suggested I put a brush in my hand, as I had happened to mention missing it. Of course there is no point putting a brush into one's hand unless she has paint to stick it into, and canvas to daub it onto, and it is much more comfortable if one has a palette so that she needn't ruin a dinner plate by using it for one. For myself, I cannot work without an easel as well, which unfortunately had to be sent from Winchester. Then there is the necessity for oils for mixing and cleaning up, and of course a smock so as not to destroy the old blue bombazine, *still* my body's only covering. The bordeaux wasn't ready yet. I believe the seamstress likes a nip in the afternoon, and will be lucky if the gown fits any better than the green shot silk did.

All told, I am now indebted to Sir Ludwig for the large sum of twenty guineas. He told me, very severely, that I am in hawk to him for close to five months' labor, which necessitated my pointing out to him he is the world's greatest nip-cheese if he paid his last governess the paltry sum of fifty guineas per annum.

"Plus room and board," he reminded me. "She didn't occupy the blue suite, however, nor have a spare chamber turned into a studio, or the salary would have been lower."

"It is news to me if a single chamber is called a *suite*—there is no dressing room attached, and as to the studio, I understood the portrait I am painting would more than cover its hire."

I was undertaking a likeness of Abigail, using a spare bedroom with a southern exposure—bad light, but not so draughty as some of the others. Its conversion to a studio consisted of no more than taking down the curtains, rolling up the carpet, and pushing the furniture against the wall. I had no real desire for him to knock out a wall or give me a larger window, but every disapproving eye turned on the renovations was met with the hint, to keep him in line. There was a fire given to us in the spartan chamber—for Abbie's benefit as she wished to be done in the guise of a nymph, wearing only the scantiest covering, a chiffon curtain it was. Actually after the first ten minutes she put on a woolen undershirt and petticoat beneath it, pretending she was cold, but she was only overly modest. Perhaps my mentioning she was a little too bulky about the midriff for a nymph had something to do with it. She had set fifteen pounds as her target for removal.

The afternoons in the studio were the most pleasant part of the day. Annie never bothered us, as she disliked the smell of my materials. Sir Ludwig also expressed the greatest aversion to them, but was frequently present all the same, complaining he could smell the paint downstairs in his study.

"You have come up here to get away from the odor, I take it?" I asked.

"No, no. I am come for my daily drubbing. You neglected to mention over lunch—being so preoccupied to see I didn't have a piece of cake—how poorly equipped you find your studio. I wanted to give you a chance to remind me."

"Consider yourself reminded. I *do* wish I had a smaller brush as well, for this bit around the mouth. You won't mind if your mouth reaches your ear on the left side, Abbie? I could not like to buy a brush for the detailed work when I was already in such deep debt to your brother."

"Do I have to keep smiling?" she asked, through a pained smile.

"No, my dear, it is not in the least necessary. I know it is a trial to all you Kesslers to tackle a smile. I should have painted you as Cassandra and had done with it."

"I suppose she is some fat goddess, is she?" Abbie asked suspiciously.

"She is the prophetess of doom."

Ludwig came around to stand at my shoulder, thus making it utterly impossible to put on a single atom of paint without making a mess. "That's very nice," he said judiciously.

"Nice is an uninformative word. Could you be more specific?"

"Surely it indicates approbation of some sort."

"Yes, but of *what*? Do you like the pose, the expression, the style?"

"Yes, yes, and yes—satisfied with all three."

"Good, then if you have no constructive criticism, perhaps you will be kind enough to get off my shoulder and let me proceed with it."

"One would take *me* for the governess," he said with ill humor, but he left us alone.

We—Abigail and I, worked on French in the mornings, did some readings of a broadening nature in English (we interpreted the term broadly, to include any novel in which we were interested), and occasionally took a turn at the pianoforte. She was the teacher here. She had exceeded my slender accomplishments and laughed quite openly when I sat down to hammer out my three tunes. Her brother's suggestion that I ought to knock a little something off my fifty guineas per annum due to this lack in my skills was met with the rejoinder that I doubted very much I would ever see a penny.

"So do I doubt it. You're into me for twenty guineas already, and you've only been with us five days. At this rate you'll have run through something in the neighborhood of fifteen hundred pounds by the end of a twelvemonth. Pass the ham, Abbie." We were having this discussion over dinner one evening.

"Your brother is a keen accountant," I complimented Abigail. "Do you suppose he might give me lessons? I never can remember whether two and two are four, or four and four are two. I'm quite sure he is cheating me, and want to check out my interest when he has calculated it."

Abbie handed me the ham for passing along without any comment on my jibe. She delighted to have me tackle her brother, but gave me little support. I set the meat down without offering it to Kessler, in a subtle effort to curb his appetite.

"Ludwig wants the ham, Rose," Annie reminded me.

"Oh, excuse me! I thought Sir Ludwig had already had some ham." I had to either give it to him then or make an issue of it. As he was regarding me with a challenging eye, I passed it.

"We'll strike a bargain," he said with a sardonic smile. "I *won't* eat another slice if you *will*. That way we will both be improving our figures."

I felt completely foolish, but also completely full. "I couldn't eat another bite."

"Rose is not too thin. Why do you say so, Lud?" Annie asked. She had allowed me to be just right in size as soon as I fell back into the habit of taking a little sugar in my tea again. "And neither are you too fat. What the devil is this nonsense? Both of you have some," she ordered. In fact, neither of us had. My hints were beginning to sink in. The night before, Sir Ludwig had refused dessert.

With such good success in all their eating, I felt the time had come to begin varying the fare offered at the table. In five days we had eaten only roast meat, always with the same pan gravy, if there was a sauce served at all. Some clever Frenchman said the English have a hundred religions and only one sauce. He was right, but the Germans have been known to do better. I had had initially some hope of tasting a meal done in the *nach Jägerart* style, served with mushrooms sautéed in a wine sauce along with other vegetables. The cook's name was Feilotter, but her way with a piece of meat was dreadfully English. Nor did she ever give us a ragoût. However, we were spared both wiener schnitzel and sauerkraut, to do her justice.

"I'm a little tired of ham myself," Abbie remarked, giving me an excellent cue.

"One does tire of the same old things. Does Mrs. Feilotter never make you up a ragoût?" I asked.

They all three stared at me as though I had suggested we eat roast rat. "We had a rabbit stew last month," Ludwig thought.

"Last month! You have the memory of an elephant," I told him.

"Elephants have need of a long memory."

"Why?" Abbie asked him.

"Well, for one thing, the gestation period is something over twenty months."

This right at table, and with three ladies for company! I scowled up the board, to see him regarding me with a lazy smile, trying to get a rise out of me. "I hadn't realized you were interested in such things, as you are still a bachelor."

"Gentlemen are always interested in the matter of begetting offspring."

"Ludwig!" Abbie howled. "Upon my word, what will Rose think of you! And you are usually so *nice* in these matters too."

"If I have offended your sense of modesty, Sister, I apologize."

"You had better apologize to Rose."

"I don't believe I have offended hers."

I tried hard to look offended. "Shocked would be more like it!" Abbie said. With my honor thus gallantly defended, I said nothing.

That interlude was fairly typical of the sort of conversations we had over dinner. There seemed little hope of bringing this crew to a sense of propriety, or of elegance, either. The meals were not changed.

The newspapers arrived at the office of the stage, and were eagerly perused by Sir Ludwig and myself when he brought them home. He became quite excited when he read a black-edge notice proclaiming that a Miss Grafton was missing from her home in Gillingham. I must say the name sent a little shiver of something through me. I snatched the paper from him and read the item through carefully. Miss Lorraine Grafton, it said, had been missing from her home since December 1, having disappeared without a trace while out for a trip to do some shopping. She was the daughter and sole offspring of Sir Rodney Grafton, heiress apparently to an estate worth close to fifty thousand pounds. Her uncle, Mr. Morley, lived with her and was her guardian, as she was an orphan. The next item nearly threw me into an apoplexy. Her late father was well known in the world of art as a collector, famed particularly for his knowledge of Italian works. "It's me! It's got to be me!" I shouted, pointing this bit out to Sir Ludwig.

He grabbed the paper back, and with our heads together we read on. Mr. Grafton had travelled extensively on the Continent amassing his storehouse of paintings. "No doubt about it!" Kessler agreed.

There was very little doubt in my own mind that I read of myself. My eyes traveled back to the first part, with the mention of fifty thousand pounds. What a happy discovery to make! I was rich! Ludwig jumped up in his excitement and ran for maps to locate Gillingham. "That place is very close to here," he told me. "Here we have been neighbors all these years and never met."

"Do you know the family at all?"

"Never heard of them. Here we are," he said, fingering a dot on the map. "Why, it's within a stone's throw of Shaftesbury! That is where the driver of the stage said you might have got on."

"The date too is just right! December 1. It was December the second when I straggled into Wickey. Imagine! I have been within forty or fifty miles of home all this time and no one has come for me!"

"The storm held up traffic for days. I knew it was nonsense you were in any trouble. A simple case of loss of memory. You had some accident, and in this state boarded a stage to Shaftesbury, then on towards Wickey."

"I wonder why I got off in the middle of the road, though?"

"Oh—in that state of confusion you didn't know what you were about. Miss Wickey told me you were completely distracted when you arrived at the rectory door."

"I had an awful feeling, though, that I didn't want to be found. With fifty thousand pounds to lure me back, wouldn't you think . . ."

"Fell says it is not at all uncommon to have these unexplained fears in such cases as yours. Sometimes too the victim doesn't want to remember. We'll find out exactly how the situation stands in Gillingham with this Morley before we let you go back. If he is trying to hustle you into doing something you dislike . . ."

I had to smile a little at this. I had no recollection of Mr. Morley, but no feeling either that I was the sort to bolt only because an uncle was trying to bearlead me—into some undesired marriage, I suppose was what he meant. "I am not a child, you know. I doubt my uncle is the reason I left."

"A young lady might well be pressured by an older relative. Fell says . . ."

"When did you discuss me with Fell and Miss Wickey?"

"What has that to say to anything?" he asked impatiently.

It indicated to me a greater concern in the affairs of a stranger than seemed likely. "Let's see what else the article has to say."

It was fairly long. We read it to the end in silence, my own silence due to a sinking sensation that it was not me written about at all. I didn't *feel* I was Miss Grafton. Surely one's own name would be instantly recognized. There was a little familiarity with the name, but it was not a strong enough association somehow. Miss Grafton had been educated at a ladies' seminary in Bath. It mentioned nothing of any travels. The last line pretty well clinched my decision. She was seventeen years old. Looking to my companion, I noticed he was regarding me in a speculative way.

"I would have taken you for a few years older," he admitted, for he knew by my face I had decided against Miss Grafton.

"I would have taken myself for *several* years older."

"Travel is broadening. Your air of sophistication makes you seem a little older than you are."

"No mention is made of any traveling. Miss Grafton has been cooped up in a seminary in Bath, which I am convinced would be the most narrowing existence possible."

"There were the summers. You might have been taken abroad with your father."

I looked back to the article for more details. "And it mentions here she is five feet four inches, too," I pointed out. I was taller.

"Approximately," he countered. "The coloring is right. Brown hair and brown eyes."

"I'm more than seventeen."

"Dammit, you're not *old*! It's impossible *two* young ladies disappeared on the same day, both mixed up in art, both from around Gillingham or Shaftesbury."

"She was an heiress. How should I be wearing this old dress if I were she?"

"It doesn't mention she was a stylish dresser."

"Oh really! As though anyone with a better gown would wear this *thing*!" I replied irritably. My anger was not really with Sir Ludwig, but due to disappointment that I was not this genteel, wealthy orphan.

"*You* are obviously a lady of some consequence, whoever you are, and you were wearing it when you strolled into Wickey."

"Who says I am a lady of some consequence? As no one has advertised for me, I am probably a governess turned off for insolence or something of the sort."

"No, no. Governesses do not lip their employers in the manner you use with me. They do not travel around the world, laugh when they destroy a good length of silk material. They would not automatically stroll down late to the family breakfast table the first day in their new position. You have never behaved in any way to indicate being a servant. Much more like a spoiled heiress. You are a lady."

"Upon my word, you make it sound like the worst sort of insult! I'm sorry if I have *lipped* you, and I did not *laugh* when I ruined the green silk. I laughed when Annie snatched it up for a shawl."

"I didn't mean to be offensive. The fact is, governesses are mousey, self-effacing women without a word to say but please and thank you. I don't know why they should behave so when they work hard and are poorly paid, and are generally well bred enough, but so it is. You have always behaved in a perfectly natural manner, to the extent that anyone can in this disordered household. I think very likely you are this Miss Grafton. We shall drive over to Gillingham and see Mr. Morley tomorrow. Don't fear we mean to quite desert you. It is fairly close—I shall return within a few days to discover how you are going on, and if there is anything amiss . . ."

"It's a waste of time. I'm not, I *know* I'm not Miss Grafton."

"No, you don't, Miss Grafton," was his answer. "In the meanwhile, I have just had another idea."

"If you mean to point out a governess would not buy oil paints . . ."

"Not that. It's Gwynne. I wouldn't be a bit surprised if he knows this Grafton girl."

"He would surely have mentioned it when I was there!"

"Oh—of course. I forgot that in the excitement of finding out who you are. He would almost certainly know her father, have known him I mean, and likely know Morley as well. It's worth a visit. I'm going to see him this instant."

He didn't invite me to go with him, and I didn't

suggest it. "You'll want to tell Abigail and Annie," he said before leaving.

I did nothing of the sort. Annie was resting, and I did the same. I went to my room and lay on the bed, to think about this latest turn in the case. How nice if I could be a perfectly respectable heiress who lived within visiting distance of Granhurst. I had come to like the place, the people. I liked even better the fifty thousand pounds. Who in her right mind wouldn't?

He was back an hour later, full of excitement. "Mr. Morley is visiting Gwynne tomorrow," he said, smiling as broadly as could be. "We'll drop over while he's there and let him see if you're his niece. Gwynne has never seen the girl at all. Knew her father as I thought, and knew he had a daughter at school, but has never met her."

"Did you think to enquire whether her father was in the habit of taking her abroad with him?"

"He wasn't. The girl has never been out of England."

I leveled a look at him. "That means nothing," he explained. He must have been thinking about it on his way home, for he had the explanation ready. "Your father would have spoken of his travels—told you vivid tales of them, no doubt. With your fertile imagination, you conjured them up into living pictures."

"Did I conjure up a rain storm outside of Schloss Ludwigsburg?"

"Why not? Oh, by the way, it's that little Italian madonna Morley is coming to see."

"I thought it was a Mr. Uxbridge who was interested in it."

"I guess Morley is interested too. Everyone seems interested in the Fra Lippi madonna."

Till it could be positively proven I was not Miss Grafton, Sir Ludwig continued to use the name to address me, and when the others were told the exciting news, they too tried to remember to address me as Miss Grafton. Abbie did not quite buy his story.

"Only two years older than I am?" she asked, surprised.

A hundred seemed more like it. I felt very old, and tired, and not at all like Miss Grafton. I did begin to think though that our stories might be connected, due to some little similarity in our backgrounds.

Chapter Six

That night, I had another of my vivid dreams. In it I saw as clear as day the Medici triptych—the central portion, that is, and the wing with the madonna, Gwynne's share of the intriguing thing. The central portion was a depiction of the Christ child in the crib, with three angels guarding Him. They were all four, Christ child and angels, quite obviously little fat-cheeked, bold Italian babies, just the sort one sees so often in Italy, with that lovely shade of hair, golden on top, darker underneath. The picture was so startlingly exact I took the notion I had actually seen it sometime, somewhere. And why should the idea fill me with that shadow of dread that I hadn't felt in two days now, dread and anger?

It put me in a peevish mood that was not improved when Sir Ludwig chose that particular day to resume wearing his monocle. I had hinted him out of it earlier on, but he stuck it into his eye as I came to the breakfast table. "Good morning, Miss Grafton," he said.

I bid a sulky good morning to the group. As you may imagine, I was on thorns to get over to Gwynne's place. Mr. Morley was not coming till afternoon, however, so that I had first to get in an interminable morning before going. Kessler had mentioned three as the hour we were to go. At two neither of us could contain curiosity longer, and we went, being sure to arrive an ill-bred half hour before we were expected. Mr. Morley was there before us, as it had been Gwynne's idea to get his business out of the way before our coming. I knew when Mr. Morley regarded me with no more than mild curiosity that I was not his niece. Sir Ludwig knew it, too, but pressed on with his enquiries all the same.

Much was made of the affair of Miss Grafton's and my own similarity of background—both young, art-interested, and so on. "My niece is a much younger girl of course," Morley said. I looked with significance to Kessler at this, letting him know he was mad to have thought me seventeen. "Less able to take care of herself. I am extremely worried about her."

He looked worried. He looked in fact like a constitutional worrier. A small, harried, worry-wart of a man, with much of the woman about him. I smiled to myself at the absurdity of my companion's thinking I should have gone in fear of this man.

"We do not fear she is dead in any case," he explained. "We suspect it is a kidnapping, as her woman was with her, and she too has vanished. We believe, the police and myself, that the companion was instrumental in having her abducted. She was new with us, you see. We didn't know all that much about her. She had credentials, a letter of character from her last employer, and it checked out all right."

"Have you received a demand for payment?" Sir Ludwig asked.

"No, not yet, but it is hardly over two weeks."

"Surely they would have been in touch with you before now!"

"Not necessarily. We do not give up hope by any means. My friends feel the first object of the kidnappers may have been to remove her well away from the district to avoid detection, and then we will hear from them. The storm has delayed everything. You don't think they'd harm her, do you?" he worried.

"How the devil should I know?" Kessler replied, with no feelings whatever for the poor man's predicament.

"What was her companion's name?" I asked.

"Miss Smith," he answered, while I shriveled into my chair.

"You should have circulated a description of her as well as your niece," Gwynne informed him.

"My friends feel it best not to antagonize the kidnappers," was the reason given for not having done so. "Not to worry them, or rush them into precipitate action."

I began to perceive that with such friends advising him Mr. Morley had no need of enemies, to use the common saw. I could see the others silently echoed my view from the stunned manner in which they regarded him. But he was worrying into his collar, and didn't observe us as we exchanged a look.

"What *did* the companion look like?" Kessler asked.

"I never saw the woman myself," he told us. "I was gone up to London to see some paintings I was having restored for my niece's collection, and the woman was hired during my absence."

"Who hired her?" Kessler demanded.

"My housekeeper—a connection of my late wife's, and an excellent, competent woman in every way. Miss Smith was hired as a companion to Lorraine. We had been looking about for someone since her coming out of the school in Bath. She needed companionship. As the woman had a good knowledge of French and art, too, we felt she might put the final touch on Lorraine's

75

French, and try to inculcate in her some appreciation of her inheritance. The woman was quite exceptional, my housekeeper said, and seemed too good to pass up, so she was hired provisionally during my absence. The solicitors gave permission. They knew I would want it done. Otherwise the woman would not have waited. She said she was in demand as a companion to young ladies."

We were then treated to a description of the inheritance, the Grafton collection, that is. I only half listened, and I noticed that Sir Ludwig was acutely uncomfortable. It had not escaped his notice that the description of the unknown companion bore a strong resemblance to myself. Even, God help me, the name I was currently using, which might very well be my own, for I had slipped into it with no trouble at all. The French, the knowledge of art, sounded dreadfully like me. And was I a kidnapper, then? Sunk from heiress to servant-kidnapper in one day?

Ludwig was clearly thinking in this groove, too. "You didn't *see* the companion, but you must have heard her described, as she is considered to be involved deeply. How did she look?"

"My housekeeper, Mrs. Lantry, described her to me. She was a youngish woman, late twenties or early thirties, she thought. Tall, well built, with darkish hair. She was very stylish, elegant. She was wearing a blue fur-lined cape on the day she disappeared, and a blue suit under it. She always dressed well, Mrs. Lantry said. Hardly dressed like a woman who had to work, but then she used to work for some wealthy French family teaching the children English, and she said her employer gave her the clothing—the fur-lined cape and so on."

"What was Miss Grafton wearing that day?" I asked, with my heart in my throat. If the man said she had been wearing the navy bombazine gown in which I sat, I was ready to hand myself over to the authorities. I was afraid I had somehow got the clothes off my victim's back.

"She wore black. She was still in mourning for her father, you must know. Died less than a year ago, and she was still in mourning for him. She was always respectful of the proprieties."

This was some small relief. Kessler arose at once and suggested we leave. I knew he wanted to get me out the door before either Morley or Gwynne tumbled to it I was the missing companion, but Morley's next speech riveted me to my chair.

"May I see the Medici madonna now?" he asked Gwynne, in a small, apologetic voice.

I had to see it again, too. I had been yearning for another look at it. We all went into the gallery, and Morley lifted it from its easel. I had an overwhelming desire to grab it from his fingers. Naturally I controlled the impulse, but it took all my will to do it.

"It certainly looks to me to match our Saint Joseph. Surely it is the other half of the door. I'll have Mr. Uxbridge stop by and take a gander next time he is passing by. He will know for sure. If the two are a pair, what price do you ask for it, Mr. Gwynne?"

"Uxbridge—was he working on *your* behalf?" Gwynne asked.

"He is my agent. He tells me he can get a better price on acquisitions if he acts for me. When the seller hears it is the Grafton people who are after a piece, they raise the price to the skies. He is very clever, Uxbridge."

"Yes, that is often done," I agreed with him.

"She is not for sale," Gwynne said firmly. "*I* wish to purchase your half."

"Oh I don't think I should sell it," Morley answered, worried of course. "Uxbridge has told me to hang on to it, and try if I can find the central portion. I leave the transactions of the gallery in his discretion, for he knows a great deal more than I do about art. He makes all sales and purchases for me."

"What, and are you selling off some of the Grafton pieces then?" Gwynne asked, startled.

"Only a few pieces Mr. Uxbridge feels are inferior, not worth holding on to."

"I don't recall any such pieces in Mr. Grafton's collection," Gwynne said at once, then with a collector's crafty greed, he quickly went on. "I would be interested to be notified if any pieces are up for sale."

"I'll speak to Uxbridge, but he has found some fellow in London who gives him a better price than he can get elsewhere. There are people with money to burn in London."

Gwynne looked disbelieving at this speech. He was also disappointed that Mr. Morley had not brought his piece of the triptych with him, as it appeared this had been the idea behind the visit, but it turned out after lengthy talk that Morley had been visiting relatives trying to decide what to do about recovering Lorraine, and did not come directly from Gillingham. He assured Gwynne he would be happy to receive him at Gillingham, and why did not *he* bring his piece when he came, that they might put them side by side to see how they matched.

They were both as jealous as mother hens of their piece of the triptych. Mr. Morley soon took his leave. I made sure Kessler would be out the door with him, but he remained behind.

"This Uxbridge is up to some monkey business," he said to Gwynne, the instant the man was gone.

"The same thought occurred to me. I know Grafton's collection, and he had no inferior pieces. All were worth keeping, and as Morley has no notion what the stuff is worth, he might be allowing himself to be bilked out of priceless masterpieces. We must look into this business, Lud."

They discussed it for a few moments, taking the decision to go to Gillingham on a fishing expedition in the near future, then we left. I saw no point in mincing words. "You can drop me off at the constable's office," I said.

"Don't be foolish."

"There's nothing foolish about it. We have discovered who I am at last. I speak French; I am traveled; I am interested in art, know a little something about it. Clearly I palmed myself off on this Mrs. Lantry as a companion to Lorraine Grafton for the purpose of kidnapping her. I have figured out my motive, too. I wanted to steal St. Joseph—her piece of the triptych. I daresay I have it stashed away somewhere, and was on my way to steal Mr. Gwynne's madonna when someone knocked me senseless."

"I can't credit you would be so ineffectual. If your motive was to steal the door, you would hardly have gone about it in such a fashion. It was there, presumably, in the Grafton gallery, to be picked up any time without kidnapping the girl."

"I have expensive tastes and habits. I wanted a little cash to go with it."

"You weren't wearing a fur-lined cape when you turned up."

"Thank God for that! And I wasn't wearing Miss Grafton's mourning outfit, either. I feared I had switched clothing with her, though I can't see why I should. Mine sounded nicer."

"Stop chattering, Rose. I'm trying to think."

"Calling me Rose Trelawney instead of Miss Smith isn't going to save me from Bridewell and very likely the gibbet."

"The companion, Miss Smith, she was older. Late twenties or early thirties, he mentioned."

"I could be a well-preserved twenty-nine or so."

"I doubt you're a day over twenty-one. Twenty-two at most."

"What should I do?" I asked.

"Stay well away from Gillingham."

"Oh, you *do* think I am the kidnapper!"

"I do not think anything of the kind. It is only an assumption that the companion abducted the girl. She, too, disappeared; kidnapped herself for all we know."

"In that case the thing to do is to confront Mrs. Lantry with me, and see if I am the companion."

"That's one way of proceeding," he allowed reluctantly.

"Can you suggest a better?"

"I should like to know who *did* snatch Miss Grafton before we go charging in. The housekeeper herself could be in on it for all we know, eager to find a victim to lay the blame on. A nice, helpless victim unable to defend herself. Then there is the mysterious Mr. Uxbridge, selling off the Grafton paintings and being held accountable to no one but Mr. Morley, so far as I can see. Who is to say Morley is innocent, for that matter? I felt his performance to be a trifle overdone. No, we don't take you there till we know a little more."

"Well, I think I *am* Miss Smith, and my only hope is that I, too, am a victim in the affair, and not the ringleader."

"There have to be *three* women. Whose cloak were you wearing? Not Miss Smith's fur-lined one; not Miss Grafton's black; and not, we think, your own. Someone else's. Mrs. Lantry's, perhaps?"

"Surely that makes at least *four* women."

He wasn't listening. "We didn't think to enquire for a description of Mrs. Lantry. But then she is not missing . . ." I went on. "Oh, dear, what a muddle it is!"

"All part and parcel of the same muddle. Same date, same place, more or less, same theme—art. You know what we might do is discover from Morley who the Smith woman's reference was. She had a character reference, and he said he checked it out, or the solicitor or someone did."

"Yes, but very likely it is some person in France. Is that not what he said, her last employer was a French family?"

"She used to work for them, I believe, is what he said. The mention of the woman's being outfitted in a higher style than one would expect—that is interesting, is it not?"

I felt it the most condemning of the lot myself. "I like pretty feathers. If I were someone's companion I would spend all my money . . ."

"Or someone's," he tossed in.

"Or someone's, on clothing, and make up an excuse to account for it. It sounds remarkably like me."

"It exceeds the bounds of probability that Miss Grafton is also suffering a loss of memory, and as she did not turn up with you, why does she not come forward, if you are her alleged abductor? What is to stop her from going home, since she has evaded your clutches?"

"I was not working alone, Sir Ludwig! I clearly had an accomplice or two."

"I wish you will be sensible and help me figure this thing out," he said brusquely, refusing to recognize the obvious.

"You're very much mistaken if you think I consider it a joking matter."

"All right then, let us discuss it rationally. Miss Grafton is missing, assumed kidnapped. She was accompanied by an unknown woman calling herself a companion, calling herself Miss Smith. That name is very likely not her own. It is the first name chosen for an alias."

"Yes, but don't you see? If her reference checked out, then she either is *really* Miss Smith, and probably innocent, or her ex-employer is in on the hoax as well."

"That's right!" he beamed. "Now we're getting somewhere. It is pretty farfetched that a perfectly respectable ex-employer of Miss Smith is involved in a vile scheme with an ex-employee. Why should a decent woman behave so? So Miss Smith is probably a victim in the thing, along with Miss Grafton. So if that's who you are, you are no kidnapper at least."

Now that we had established Miss Smith in a semblance of respectability in this arbitrary fashion, I was allowed to be she. "It still doesn't explain my clothing, or what I was doing getting off the stage in the middle of nowhere."

"They might have drugged you. Whoever kidnapped Miss Grafton had *you* to contend with—no small problem. They doped you enough to make you groggy, put you on the stage, and in a stupor you stumbled off when you began to come to. Your memory was gone."

"That seems a very temporary way to have dealt with me. Who was to say I would lose my memory? It doesn't explain my clothing, either."

"They needed a good warm fur-lined cape for the Grafton girl—it was December, and with a longish trip planned . . ."

"I thought that part of Morley's story particularly absurd. And would they have taken my blue suit, too? What about those black shoes, half an inch too long, so unsuitable to an elegant fur-lined cape as well."

All my objections began to form a wedge in his credulity. "Does it seem plausible to you you might have been a companion? I must confess it is not the background I envisaged for you when first we met."

"It doesn't feel at all like me, but then Miss Smith is a strange creature. She didn't dress like a hired companion, and I doubt she acted like one either. Even her getting herself the post when the man who ought to have been hiring her was away makes her sound very bossy and intrusive, and you must own I am not unlike that. She wormed her way into the young Grafton girl's good graces." And had not *I* been at pains to wind Abigail around my thumb?

"No," he said firmly, having leapt to another unfounded conclusion. "You were right in saying you are not seventeen, and *I* am right in saying you are not some ten years older. You are neither Miss Grafton nor Miss Smith. So we shall cease calling you by those names, Rose."

"Oh dear, I suppose I am Rose Trelawney again, am I?"

"Why not? It's a nice romantical name, as Annie

said, and you become more romantical by the day. I wonder what we will find out about you next."

"We haven't found out a single, solitary thing yet."

"We have found out you're not Miss Grafton and decided you are not Miss Smith. *I* have found out a few other things as well," he added with a quite unnecessary note of derision in the last sentence. Then he stuck his monocle in his eye, and found out I was not beneath telling him to kindly remove it, or I would walk the rest of the way home.

Chapter Seven

I perhaps gave you too grand an idea of Granhurst by mentioning a similarity to Schloss Ludwigsburg. It was only that the front of the entire building belonging to Kessler bore some intentional resemblance to the *corps-de-logis* of the original. There were no pavilions attached, certainly nothing in the nature of the luxurious game-room or *Jagdpavillion*, no enclosed courtyard in which one might with ease parade an infantry division as at Ludwigsburg. It was not of such imperial proportions. In fairness to Sir Ludwig, I must confess that I searched in vain too for a replica of that debauched *cabinet d'amour* designed for Duke Eberhard Ludwig, with its shocking nudes done in bas-relief and all those mirrors in strategic places. The ancestors of Sir Ludwig were too English for that, or their wives were.

Due to my arriving at the place in December, I got about the parks and gardens very little. They were still ankle-deep in wet snow and not attractive in that season, but there was one feature I intended to investigate, snow or not. This was a chapel. I thought when first I espied it from Abigail's room that Granhurst was built on the ruins of some older home, but it was not the case. The chapel was not what remained of some abbey or castle; it was a folly built by the second owner to lend the place a touch of class and give it a spurious air of history. I was curious to see what sort of a mess it was inside. I envisioned some duplicate of the bad taste to be found within the walls of the home proper.

As I was treated in every way as quite an honored guest, though to be sure one who had hurled at her head with monotonous regularity how much money she owed her host, I did not feel myself to be encroaching to ask Sir Ludwig if I might see the place. I did not ask him on the same day as we went to meet Mr. Morley. We were all too busy discussing the niche I might hold in the case for the thought to enter my head. The next day the weather turned quite bad again. We were fearing a repeat of the blizzard of two weeks before, and Sir Ludwig put off his trip to Gillingham on that account. I was quite simply amazed when he refused to let me see the chapel.

"Not now," was his reply, expressed with a certain impatience. "I'm busy, Rose."

"I didn't mean to ask you to accompany me. I wanted only to get the key, that I might have a look around for myself," I explained.

"No, I don't think that's a good idea."

"Why not?"

"Because I don't," was his unrevealing answer. German!

"Have you got something to hide?"

"Yes. *You.*"

He had been curt enough the last day that I did not press the matter further. He seemed preoccupied, worried. Since the visit with Mr. Morley, in fact, I had been treated with a certain brusqueness at definite odds with my former treatment. It seemed Sir Ludwig had taken the idea that as I was not a missing heiress, I was indeed her kidnapper. He had hotly denied it, but a cooler consideration had given rise to doubts. He feared he was entertaining a criminal, and his eagerness to get over to Gillingham without me to check it out made him irascible. A dozen times he cursed the falling snow, with a quite careless disregard for the presence of three females. He was snappish not only with me but with Annie and Abigail as well. Nor did he join us in the studio as he used to. It seemed strangely empty without him there bothering the life out of us.

It was a great relief when the next morning showed us clear skies, and no more than an inch of snow fallen, fast melting, so that the trip was at last possible. Abbie, who was a bit of a road hog, asked to go with him.

"You will want to stay and keep Rose company," he told her.

As she obviously wanted nothing of the sort, I encouraged her to go. It would be easier to get into the chapel without her along. As if reading my mind, Sir Ludwig turned to me before leaving and said, "We'll see the chapel tomorrow. I have the key with me. I want you to stay home and do nothing foolish."

It was of all things he could have done and said the most likely to precipitate folly on my part. There was even an urge to break the chapel lock, but of course I could not go quite that far. I must contrive other mischief. Annie undertook to amuse me in the morning, by a tour of the house. There was hardly a nook of it I had not been into already. With some interest in architecture, it was not to be supposed I had not long since got into all unlocked chambers except the master bedroom. I got in there that morning. How I longed to be at it, rearranging the furniture, stripping the yellowing paper from the walls and putting up new, removing those great heavy pieces and putting in better ones that stood unseen and unused in bedrooms seldom occupied by any guests. In the gold guest suite on the east corner, for instance, sat a perfectly beautiful Queen Anne desk and matching chair, while the master of the house used a scratched mahogany that might have been hammered together by himself, for any aesthetic value it had. Worst of all was that I could not even chide him about it, for I had no idea of announcing what I had been doing, unless Annie blurted it out. Far from impossible, but I counted on her faulty memory.

Next we went to the attics, where I had not earlier ventured, to see that finer furnishings were stored as lumber than graced many of the saloons belowstairs. I could not bring myself to leave up in the dark a satinwood cabinet, Hepplewhite I judged from the straight legs and other details, with delicate *pietra-dura* panels inlaid on the front doors. "Why do you not have that pretty thing taken down to the main Saloon, Annie?" I asked her.

"Ruth never liked it," she told me.

Ruth, I had already learned, was Abbie's mother. She seemed a special deity of Annie's, often quoted, so that I saw some trouble talking her into bringing it down. It was my intention to place it in lieu of the heavy Kent chest presently forming the focal point of the Saloon. Whether half a dozen stout footmen could ever get the Kent monstrosity up these narrow stairs was a moot point, but they could surely get it out of the Saloon at least, and lose it in some dark corner, of which there were many.

By a series of judicious compliments on the panels, I soon convinced her Ruth could not have had the poor taste to dislike this particular piece. It was the old Kent one in the Green Saloon Ruth detested. She was furious with Ludwig then for having defied his mother's wishes in removing this one from below. She even set on the occasion when he had done it in spite over some detail in the woman's will. Giving Annie five hundred pounds, I believe it was. I had to tread warily to make her see it was only forgetfulness on Ludwig's part that had caused him to be so callous, for I didn't want a full-scale war on my hands. I needed him in a good mood, and he hadn't been recently. The thing was done in jig time. It was the smallness of Annie's bequest that had triggered his anger. Kent was consigned to a corner of the study, a nice dark corner so that it need not be too frequently seen. The Hepplewhite was a vast improvement to the Saloon, except that its delicate lines and coloring rendered more jarring those hideous hunter-green draperies and more insipid the salmon-pink rug. After a few repetitions, Annie tumbled to it she was to disapprove of these two items, and before long she announced, "I shall make Lud change them. See if I don't! The place was used to be much more stylish when Ruth was alive."

Ruth, I assumed, must have gone to her maker some several years ago, for that carpet had been without nap for a decade.

"We'll see if we can't get it done in time for the New Year's party," she said. "A party makes a dandy excuse for a bit of trimming up. We don't often have a party since Ruth is gone, which is why we have fallen into rack and ruin; (perhaps I ought not to have used such a strong phrase for her to repeat). But at New Year's, at least we have a do."

Christmas was fast approaching. It was past mid-December already, the twentieth. To get these things done by New Year's would take fast footwork. Annie went for her nap after luncheon, and I went to the park, looking for more mischief to get into. I spotted holly bushes and greenery to be culled later for trimming the house. Before long my feet were heading to the chapel, where my heart had been directing them all along. It was set off several hundred yards from the house, in a clearing. The door was locked, but I took a good look around the exterior. Granhurst was in yellow stone, like its ancestor. The chapel was gray. There was nothing German about it. A would-be Romanesque thing it was—low, rounded windows and recessed Romanesque doorway with some not exceptional carvings decorating the curves. The door was locked, and I knew where the key was. At Gillingham. I might have trouble talking away the Hepplewhite cabinet without a smashed lock, so I abandoned thoughts of getting inside.

I strolled around to the rear, having some trouble walking in Annie's pattens that were a good inch too short. That was where it happened, behind the chapel, well concealed from the house. I heard a sound as of bushes rustling and hurried footsteps. The bushes moving led me to suspect a dog was loose. Granhurst might have been called "Doghurst" for the number of hounds and other canines Ludwig kept. I suspect from the quantity of dog hairs to be found on sofas and padded chairs that, prior to my arrival, they might have had the run of the Saloon, and of course I already knew the spaniel's toilet habits. The footfalls, however, were louder than those of a dog. They were human, and stealthy. Strangely enough, I felt no fear. I was often overcome with a tide of panic for no reason, but now, when reason was there, I felt only that some maid was sneaking out to meet her beau. Bess I selected for the culprit, as she was the prettiest of the household girls.

Curiosity, one of my besetting sins, urged me to confirm my suspicion. I was in no position, nor mood for that matter, to chide her, but I wished to see who she had taken for a lover that I might twit Sir Ludwig about competition. Not that he flirted with her, actually, but she was inordinately pretty and I occasionally accused him of debauching his servants as he prided himself a little on sailing a taut ship. I went along to the back of the building, in time to see a leg disappear around the corner. Bess was flying high. It was a well-polished gentleman's boot I got a passing glimpse of.

This promised to be rather embarrassing. If some prestigious neighbor of Kessler's was carrying on with a housemaid, I was not particularly eager to be aware of it. I stood undecided a moment, really considering how to get away without being seen. The best way was to just return to the house as though I had heard or seen nothing, and I turned around to do so. Moving at an awkward gait because of the pattens—the old-fashioned kind with metal rings—I was slow to escape. I had not quite reached the front of the chapel when I was felled by a blow from behind. Not a hard enough blow to knock me unconscious, but enough to stun me. My pursuer had moved quickly and silently to overtake me. I fell forward, but broke the fall with my hands. By the time I reached my feet again, hollering at the top of my lungs, my assailant was gone—run back behind the church and off into the spinney beyond. Much as I would have liked to see who he was, I had not the intention of going after him. I ran back to the house as fast as I could, to find my call had been unheard. Bess was busy in the Saloon polishing the cabinet we had had brought down.

She was humming happily to herself, and looking remarkably pretty in her mobcap, with her big blue eyes twinkling merrily, and her cheeks rosy. The homey aroma of turpentine and beeswax—not one too commonly smelled at Granhurst I confess sadly—was so mundane and reassuring that I knew Bess was innocent of any part in the affair. "Oh, you took a tumble, Miss Rose!" she said, looking at my bedraggled cape. "Let me take that to the kitchen to clean up for you." I put off my bonnet and cape, and decided to say nothing of my adventure, at least to the servants.

"How fine the cabinet looks," I complimented her. You can get a deal more work out of servants, and more happily, too, with praise than scolding.

"Sure and it's a grand improvement over that great heavy dark box that's stood here in times gone by. A shame it is the way we're sinking into commonness here at Granhurst. What we need is a mistress, a *proper* mistress I'm meaning." She smiled pertly at me as she made this remark.

She was usually a well-behaved girl, but I took the

idea this speech was a slur on my own lack of propriety. Her meaningful little look suggested it was myself
she saw as the mistress, and it seemed amazingly
impertinent for her to suggest I was improper. "Miss
Annie is getting that old and odd in her notions," she
rattled on, making her meaning clearer. I blushed
under her knowing look, and hardly knew whether I
felt more angry or foolish. To set her in her place, I
suggested that as she had her rags and materials at
hand, a touch of polish to the other pieces in the room
would not go amiss. She took this hint well, considering
it came from a governess.

Before leaving, I decided to pose one last question to
her. "Are any of the girls in this house seeing a beau,
Bess, a gentleman?"

"You're wide awake on all suits, Miss Rose. They've
never said a word to a soul, but if Millie, the upstairs
maid, hasn't had an offer from the head groom! They'll
be making the announcement at Christmas if Sir Ludwig
permits it."

"How nice for them," I said, "but I meant a *gentleman*."

"What, a real *gentry* gentleman you mean? Lord, no,
Miss. There's no carry-on of that sort with us girls. Sir
Ludwig takes a dim view of philandering. He's not a
hard master, but about that he is strict. Why were you
asking, if I may be so bold, Miss?"

"I thought I saw a gentleman skulking about the
grounds just now."

"Isn't that an odd thing, then? I thought the same
myself as I was coming down the stairway half an hour
ago. I took the idea I saw a horse cutting through the
park, but as no one came to the door, I collect it was
only a dog or a branch moving. Should I send some boys
out to have a look, then?"

"No, he would be gone by now."

To minimize talk and my own investigation of the
church from which I had been hinted away, I said
nothing to Annie either when she came down from her

rest. I wore a slight bump on the back of my head. Not so large as my former egg, but no doubt Annie would have liked to see it. Unfortunately, she was mistaken in thinking a second blow would bring my memory, which she would go on calling my mind, back in a rush. I remembered nothing I had forgotten before.

Chapter Eight

I sat in all innocence helping Annie hem up the remains of my green silk to wear as a shawl when Sir Ludwig and Abbie returned from Gillingham. "Well, and did you have a nice trip?" Annie asked.

The smile, denoting that they had, faded from Sir Ludwig's face as he spotted the satinwood cabinet sitting where it shouldn't. "What's that thing doing down here? Where's the mahogany cabinet?" he asked, darting an accusing eye to me. I sat with my lips closed and let Annie do the explaining.

"It's stuck off in the study. I had this one carted down as it was always a great favorite of Ruth's. I don't see why you must go sticking it off in the attics and fill the house up with lumber."

"I want this taken out," he said, but was diverted from more attack by an eagerness to get on with an account of his visit. He waited only to order tea before doing so. Despite the German name, the family consumed the customary English gallon of tea apiece each day. He took up a seat beside me and opened his budget.

"We can dismiss the notion that you are Miss Smith," was his opening remark. I hardly knew whether this were good or bad. "Her description does not sound like you in the least. We had one from Mrs. Lantry, the housekeeper. Miss Smith was an older woman—at least thirty from the way she was described, and she had a mole on her left cheek."

"It might have been a patch made to resemble a mole, for purposes of disguise," I mentioned.

"No, no, we have completely abandoned the idea you are Miss Smith. There were other things—wrinkles, crowsfeet, a crooked tooth."

"Good God, she sounds more like fifty than thirty. How did Mr. Morley come to describe her as a youngish woman of elegance?"

"I fancy it was the clothing led him astray. Miss Smith is not described as ugly, however. The mole was not disfiguring. We had to pose several questions before it came up at all, and the teeth were not markedly crooked. Under repeated questioning, Mrs. Lantry mentioned that one jutted a little forward, and the wrinkles and crowsfeet were spoken of as beginning. There were enough little differences that we are convinced she is not you."

"What of her character reference? Was it a French address?"

"No, the last employer was from Scotland, actually. A Mrs. Knightsbridge at Edinburgh. We saw her letter."

The image of those Scottish highlands and sheep loomed in my mind. Scotland sounded significant. I frowned over the name Knightsbridge. It rang some little bell. I disliked the name intuitively. "What did the letter say?"

"It said, apparently, just what Miss Smith had already said. She was hired as companion to Mrs. Knightsbridge. The lady is director of some small museum in Edinburgh, the Knightsbridge Museum, founded by her husband. A hobby for the wife, I suppose. The two women were active in tending to the place. Mrs. Lantry says this Miss Smith was very knowledgeable about art."

"We knew art had something to do with it. It always keeps cropping up."

"It has cropped up higher than that. Gwynne was with me, as you know. He busied himself looking around while I quizzed the woman, and he claims two valuable paintings are missing from the Grafton collection. A portrait of a woman by Titian, and some religious painting by Hans Memling—I forget the name of it. The latter he might conceivably have traded as he was getting into the Italian school in a big way, but not the Titian. *And*," he raised a finger to stop me from speaking, as he had more news to impart, "more interesting still, our mysterious Miss Smith claimed one of the works hanging there was a forgery. Now, the way that came up is as follows. Gwynne had been there before of course and particularly admired a small work attributed to Giorgione. Not positively identified—the fellow hasn't got more than a handful actually verified as his work, but this one was a likely applicant. He asked to see it, and found it had been hung in a little saloon, out of the main collection. After a single glance at it, he asked Mrs. Lantry if the original had been sold and a copy made. It had not, or not with the family's knowledge, at least. When Morley finally arrived—he was out when we got there—he said no, the painting had been sent to London for some expert to examine, but it was declared not to be a Giorgione, thus its exclusion from the collection. Gwynne is ready to swear the picture presently there is not the one he saw a year ago."

"Did Morley take it to London himself for examination?"

"No, Uxbridge took it. It was away three weeks— plenty of time for a copy to have been made, and even 'aged' with a coat of dark varnish or some such thing.

Uxbridge also arranged for the sale of the two paintings —the Titian and Hans Memling. Told Morley they were not up to the standards of the rest of the collection. The price got for them was mentioned, and Gwynne says it is a ridiculously small figure. Now it seems to me that if Miss Smith was going to point out to Morley he was being duped when he got back from his visit, it is Miss Smith and not Miss Grafton who was the one Uxbridge actually wanted to be rid of."

"You have decided Uxbridge is the villain, have you?"

"Oh yes, sight unseen. He must be. He has been cheating the Grafton estate. Gwynne says there is not a doubt of it, and he has warned Morley to beware of any further dealings with the fellow. Uxbridge lives at Shaftesbury. We went along to his place to pump him, but he is away on business. In London for an unspecified period of time, we were told."

"I wonder if it was wise to warn him you are on to him."

"I wonder too, but I was overwhelmingly eager to get a look at him, and he would have learned from Morley soon enough that he was under suspicion. Morley is in the boughs over the affair, and has run off this very day to a magistrate to press charges. He fears—you know what a worrier he is—that *he* will end up in the dock himself for negligence in the matter. It came out after a good deal of frowning and nail-biting that this is not the first intimation he has had that Uxbridge is suspicious. There were enquiries from the chap who purchased the two paintings that were sold. Rather pressing enquiries I take it from Morley's state, but Uxbridge talked his concern away. Said it was standard procedure, to make enquiries, I mean."

I listened to all of this, then asked, "Has Morley received any demand for payment in the kidnapping of his niece? Whoever abducted her has had ample time to get her and himself safely hidden."

"No, he hasn't. It begins to look as though he's mistaken about kidnapping being the motive."

"Yes, silencing Miss Smith is more like it."

"I shouldn't forget Miss Grafton is a great heiress," Abbie joined in. "The house was *luxurious*. She must be rich as Croesus, and someone must inherit all that if she is dead. I wonder who would be the heir."

"Morley," Sir Ludwig answered. "Must be. He is her closest relative by a long shot."

"Oh dear, I am convinced *he* would not want the worry of it," I said.

"If you could have seen him, close to tears, you would know he is innocent," Ludwig assured me. "He couldn't be that good an actor."

"So it seems Miss Smith's arrival at the Grafton home worried someone enough he had to be rid of her. Uxbridge is the one who was tampering with the collection, so it must be Uxbridge we are looking for. A close neighbor, he might have engineered it easily enough, but what has he done with the two women? Three weeks tomorrow since they have been missing. It begins to look . . ."

"Yes, it looks as though they are long buried," Sir Ludwig said bluntly. "And if that is the case, Uxbridge has probably got himself clean out of the country."

"In which case we will *never* discover what happened to Miss Grafton and Miss Smith!" I frowned over this, then began to wonder how *I* fit into this puzzle. I seemed to be an extra piece. The plot was complete without me. I soon realized Sir Ludwig was scanning the same riddle.

"There was no mention of any *other* young lady in the case," he said, regarding me closely. Then he hunched his shoulders and said with enthusiasm, "So, let's hear *your* news." He looked at me expectantly.

My eyes flew guiltily to the satinwood cabinet, but I soon realized it was more important news he waited to hear. His eager, expectant face said so. Impossible he had learned of my attack at the chapel!

"Who was the man enquiring after you at the rectory?" he went on, to make his point clear.

I looked at him stupidly. "What do you mean? I heard nothing of that."

"Why, Mulliner told us when we went to pick up your gown that a gentleman had been asking after you this morning. I made sure he had been here long since. A middle-aged fellow he said, a gentleman, came to the door claiming he had heard your story as far away as Bath, and had come to enquire after you. His daughter, it seems, had taken off towards the end of November. The family suspected a runaway match with a captain, but as nothing was ever heard from the couple, he began to wonder if you might be she. The name, incidentally, was Miss Smith," he added ironically.

"Another Banbury tale, then! No man came here."

"Now that is very odd, for Mulliner told him your description, and he said it sounded like his daughter, and he was coming here immediately to see you."

"He didn't come," I said. Then I gave a sudden lurch of intuition. Oh but he had come—had hit me instead of talking to me. Ludwig's eyes were examining me closely, missing nothing of my reasoning.

The tea was upon us. I decided first I would wait and tell Sir Ludwig my tale in private, but as privacy seemed hours away, I could contain it no longer. I told the story, and he jumped to his feet, upsetting the tea over his knees and the carpet.

"I told you to behave!" he shouted, as though I were seven years old.

"I *did* behave! All I did was to go out for a walk in the park, and I ran away as soon as I knew someone was there."

"It was the fellow who was asking after you at Mulliner's."

Annie was furious with me. "Do you mean to tell me, Rose Trelawney, that you have got another crack on

100

the head and didn't tell me!" she shrieked. She too hopped up, rescuing her tea before it hit the carpet, though the green silk got a splatter. She descended on me like a vulture, her claws scratching at my scalp for evidence of the attack. She was delighted when she found it. "Ah, this is a dandy one," she told Ludwig, who had then to add his fingers to my hair to feel for himself. Abbie could not be left out of such good sport, and she too came to admire my acquisition.

"If you don't mind!" I said, shaking them all out of my hair and trying to retrieve it into its bun. The effort was unsuccessful. It was tumbled well and good about my ears, and there it stayed till our meeting was over, being frequently disturbed by Annie, who couldn't get enough of feeling the bump.

"For God's sake leave the girl alone," Kessler shouted at her, then proceeded thinking aloud in a milder tone. "All hogwash, then, this tale of a runaway match," he said, with, I thought, a certain note of satisfaction. "It was Uxbridge, or someone working for him."

"It can't be that. I have nothing to do with the Grafton affair," I reminded him.

"Who could it have been?" Abbie wondered. "If you're not mixed up with the Grafton business, why would anyone want to hurt you?"

"I must be mixed up in some other mess," I suggested.

"It was your captain come after you," Annie told me. "You have given him the slip, minx, and he is jealous you're here with Lud. Ha, and if Lud ain't scowling at me like a Turk."

"I wonder if the captain's name was Ivor," he said, looking at me with a question.

I hadn't a notion, but to tell the truth, it sounded as rational as anything else, except that it was supposedly my father who enquired at Mulliner's, and my captain who knocked me on the head. We discussed all manner of improbable imbroglios in which I was mixed up, till Sir Ludwig brought us to attention, just at the point where Annie had me switching my affections from a captain to a colonel.

"This is nonsense. There are too many similarities in the Grafton affair and Rose's for them not to be connected. The art, and the time and place. The fellow needed some story to account for his enquiry and invented a captain and a runaway bride." On only one point we were in agreement. There existed no doubt in anyone's mind that the boot of which I had had a glimpse belonged to a gentleman who *said* he had come from Bath.

I was handed my bordeaux gown picked up in the village and told by my host to put it on for dinner. This gave rise to an immediate desire to leave it for another occasion, but in the end I was so curious to see how it looked that I did put it on. It fit well enough, but was a hard color to wear, and not the optimum choice for me. It made me look older, I thought. Also it was just a trifle snug, revealing somewhat more precise details of my anatomy than I usually paraded in public. When both Sir Ludwig and Annie showered me with compliments, I was sure it was in the worst of taste, but still it was no worse than the navy bombazine. I really didn't feel it merited such attention as Kessler was granting it, especially from the waist up. Half a dozen times I caught him surveying it closely, and took the notion he was looking right through it. He wore an unaccustomed little smile, and looked sheepish when I twice caught him out at it.

After dinner, the subject of the satinwood cabinet came to the fore, and we all settled in for a battle royal. "Let's get this thing out of here before we sit down," Sir Ludwig suggested with a challenging look in my direction.

Annie's blue eyes snapped. She walked forward and placed her little body before it, with her arms outstretched to protect it. "Ruth always liked it, and it must stay," she declared in dramatic accents.

"Mama could never stand the sight of it, as it was a

gift from Cousin Valerie. That is precisely the reason it was taken upstairs."

"Who was Valerie?" I asked, hoping to divert them.

"My father's first fiancée, who married another cousin and gave this cabinet as a wedding gift."

"She had excellent taste," I said, walking to the cabinet to point out the panels.

"She had the poor taste to break an engagement with my father," Ludwig countered.

"I do not refer to judgment, Sir Ludwig, but aesthetic taste merely," I answered discreetly, wishing to conciliate him. "These *pietra-dura* panels are exquisitely done, are they not?" I pointed hopefully to reproductions of scenes from classical antiquity, a brace of columns set amidst Hellenic shrubbery, a rendering of Venus on a pedestal.

"Was this *your* idea?" he asked in an accusing tone.

"It was *my* idea!" Annie insisted, "and you're quite wrong about Valerie. She gave Ruth a silver teapot, which Ruth in spite promptly put on the kitchen table for the servants. There it sits to this very day, black as the ace of spades, for no one ever polishes it."

"I think the cabinet is lovely," I pressed on. "It lightens the air of this room remarkably. The Kent cabinet was so very dark and heavy."

"I like furniture dark and heavy," Ludwig asserted with a mulish set to his jaw. "Substantial," he added, by way of explanation.

"What do you think, Abbie?" I asked, for he was fond of his sister.

"I think it's ugly," she disappointed me by saying. "The other is worse though," she added to her brother.

Kessler continued to observe the thing as best he could through Annie's body. She added nothing to its beauty I can tell you. "It's too small, too flimsy," he complained, tossing up his hands in disdain. "It makes the rest of the room look old and heavy."

Noticing his eyes flickering to the draperies, I took a deep breath and adopted a voice as disinterested as I could make it. "With lighter draperies—rose or gold, perhaps—the cabinet would look less outstanding, less out of place, I mean."

He seemed to be regarding the effects of that deep breath on my body. I thought at first he wasn't listening at all, but he soon answered, "Yes, but we don't have pink or yellow draperies. We have green."

"I didn't say pink or yellow. I said rose or gold."

"A rose by any other name is usually pink," he insisted.

"I always did hate those old dark green curtains," Abbie said, glancing at them. No more than her brother, I don't believe she even realized they were green till the discussion's beginning.

"We'll put up new curtains when we change the carpet," Annie said, darting forward from the cabinet. "It can all be done in time for the New Year's party."

"I don't plan to have the annual party this year," Ludwig said.

All talking of furniture was deflected to a tirade from the two regular female residents upon this announcement. I had to hold in all my regret. Worried looks to myself told me *I* was the cause of cancelling the party. I hastened on to assure them all I had no objection to it.

"Everyone will be gawking at you and asking questions," Ludwig told me. I took the idea he would have liked pretty well to have the party, which informed me it was a long-standing tradition, for in general he was not much of a party goer. Even fewer people than usual had been coming lately. I had discovered from little comments let drop accidentally that this was in deference to my being amongst them, but I would not have objected to company. I was more of an excuse than a reason in Kessler's thinking.

"I can stay abovestairs if that is all that's stopping you," I offered magnanimously, having, I must own, not the least intention of missing a moment of the do.

"Oh everyone will want to see *you*, Rose," Annie

assured me. "The party will be the best ever, with you to show to everyone. We never had such an interesting guest before. We had Lud's cousin that had been in debtor's prison once, but he was a dull dog after all. All the excitement occurred after he had left and taken a dozen place settings of silver with him. Pity the bump will be all gone down. Maybe we could give you a little tap . . ."

"You see what I mean," Ludwig hastened in, trying to drown her out. "You would have a stream of guests in your boudoir, feeling your bump and giving it a twin."

"Ha, and then there was the year Marion got drunk!" Annie rambled on, smiling broadly. "Cast up her accounts all over the . . ."

"Never mind, Annie!" Ludwig said in a grim voice.

"I don't see why Miss Rose need stay abovestairs," Abbie said. "Everyone in the village and for miles around has already seen her. At a party with dancing, they will have other things on their minds."

"Carousing and sluicing and flirting," Annie agreed. "I can hardly wait. If Marion pukes on the new carpet I'll box her ears."

"I leave it up to you ladies," Sir Ludwig said, knowing full well we would rush on with plans for the party, "but I think it should be cancelled."

"Good. What do you plan to do about replacing the curtains and rug, then?" Annie demanded. "We can't let anyone into such a place of rack and ruin. When will you buy them?"

"In about ten years," he replied, glancing with satisfaction at the mouldy draperies and thin carpet.

"Ludwig!" she shouted. "Take a look at this carpet. Look at it!" He glanced down, with very little interest. "It's threadbare!" she yelled.

"Nonsense, it is a trifle faded."

"It's full of holes, is what it is." Annie got down on her hands and knees to stick a finger under surface threads, which ought to have had half an inch of wool on top of them. She broke a couple in the process, forming indeed a hole where her fingers invaded the underweave. "See that! Holes!"

He looked a little more closely. "It can be turned," he decided.

"It's shabby, Lud," Abbie took it up. "It should have been replaced years ago."

"Why didn't you replace it then?" he asked, his tone becoming quite noticeably German, which is to say shouting. "I have enough to do looking after the farms and stables and orchard, without worrying about a damned carpet."

"And the drapes?" Annie asked, advancing towards them with her poking fingers, ready to invent holes if she could not find any.

"I don't want *pink* curtains," he decreed stubbornly. As he was capitulating so far, I don't see why he could not have done it with a little better grace. But then the Germans are too closely allied to their English cousins to take defeat lightly. The French hide their spleen better, I think, and the Italians can manage to make you think you've done them a favor by beating them in an argument. Of course, I don't recall ever arguing with a *female* Italian.

"I hope you're satisfied," he said, looking daggers at me.

"I?" I asked, my face a mask of astonishment. "What has all this to do with me?"

"It is odd no one noticed the disarray of the room before your arrival."

"So it is. I am convinced its disarray must have been outstanding for some several years before my coming. But if the refurbishing were *my* idea, you must know I would have begun with the paintings. I would have removed Messrs. Stubbs and Gainsborough and replaced . . ."

"No!" He stomped from the room with a wrathful eye to the satinwood cabinet. I thought he was gone to his study to sulk, but it turned out he was only changing out of his tea-stained trousers. An unaccustomed fit of dandyism on his part, or more likely an excuse for his returning so soon. At this point we women found it wise to discuss other things than the redoing of the Saloon. We had pretty well agreed on our decor during his absence, especially rose draperies, which would not be called pink by any of us. We played a hand of cards that evening, the first time we had done so. I was rather good at it, and so was Abbie. It was both unfortunate and unfair that the two worse players should get matched to take us on, but it was an amusing and lively game for all that.

It was Abbie's idea to play for rose curtains, as a sort of joke to humor the German back into smiles. As this went down with no ill humor, I placed a bid on one of the Stubbs, and had ousted them both along with Gainsborough before the evening was over, at which time we were reminded the game had only been in fun. Sir Ludwig repeated several times that Annie was in league with us against him.

"Ha, I haven't played cards in an age," she excused herself. "I'm becoming addle-pated, like Rose." She smiled so sweetly on me that it was impossible to take offense.

In fact, in spite of all the bickering and arguing that went forth in the house, it was by no means an unpleasant atmosphere. It was homey—I was treated like a member of their small family, and acted like one. No formality survived beyond the first few days. I suppose that is why I was happy, despite my predicament, and why the days flew past so quickly. Annie never stayed up late. Soon she was yawning and taking her leave of us. As soon as she was gone, Kessler said to Abbie it was time for her to go, too, as she must be tired from her trip. Since it was perfectly clear he wanted some privacy with me, I did not make the missish suggestion of going with her.

"What is it you want?" I asked when we were alone.

"I'm worried about this fellow who was hanging

around the grounds today and asking questions in the village. I don't want you out alone, not even in the gardens or park. I'll go into Wickey tomorrow and speak to Mulliner again, ask around at the inn and see if I can find out anything about him. I wish you will try to remember if there is anything might help us. This story about the captain, for instance. Do you think there's anything in it?"

"I couldn't tell you what Bath looks like, and I seem to remember *places*. Certain details of buildings and so on, I mean. I dream sometimes about Scotland. You mentioned that Miss Smith's last post was there."

He nodded, considering this. "Do you think you might come from there?"

"I don't know. In my dream it was the highlands and sheep, not Edinburgh. And there was a kitten, too."

"Not much help," he said.

"No, except that Kitty . . . Oh, it's nothing. It is just that a couple of times I called Miss Wickey Kitty."

"It sounds rather like it—the same sort of a sound, I mean."

"Yes, it does."

"Does the name Knightsbridge sound familiar at all?"

"I don't like the name."

"*Liking* it is not the point. Does it seem familiar?"

"I suppose I would not have taken it in irrational dislike if I had never heard it before."

"Possibly you know Mrs. Knightsbridge, then, and have reason to dislike her."

"Possibly. I wonder if Ivor . . . You didn't happen to ask the name of Mrs. Knightsbridge's husband?"

"She signs herself Mrs. J.F. Knightsbridge. Wrote a very pretty letter, praising Miss Smith to the skies, her industry, knowledge, agreeable temperament. Making it quite unlikely Miss Smith is yourself," he added in a bantering way.

"We had already agreed the mole and crooked tooth invalidated my claim to the name, had we not?"

"Mmm, and the wrinkles and crowsfeet."

He seemed in some danger of falling into admiration of my new gown again, so I recalled him to business. "I wish I could get over to Gillingham and see the Grafton place. Oh, did you see the other door of the Medici triptych?"

"Yes, Gwynne was all excited about it. Seems to think old Cosimo himself might have been the model for Saint Joseph. He is more than ever convinced the doors are a matching pair."

"What did Saint Joseph look like? Why did Gwynne think Cosimo posed?"

"Had a pointy nose and a protruding chin."

"That sounds like Cosimo, all right. I wish I could see it."

"Yes, a pity we daren't risk taking you there, for they have an open house on Monday morning, and will give an interested party a guided tour of the gallery almost any time, with a little notice."

"As Mrs. Lantry's story proves I am not Miss Smith, would it not be possible for me to go?"

"I don't like it. Someone is after you. It might be someone connected with that place—a servant or what have you. I feel strongly your story is wound up with the Grafton business. Till we find out who you are, I would rather keep you under close wraps here. Whoever you are, and whatever you are involved in, you seem to be in danger. The fellow who struck you down, who knows what he might have done if he had succeeded in knocking you completely unconscious? Ladies have a way of vanishing in this affair. We don't want *you* to disappear."

"I begin to wonder you don't. I am a shocking nuisance to you. Battening myself on total strangers."

"Nonsense, we have never had such a romantical visitor before. Jailbirds and female drunkards were our most entertaining guests till you came along. We are all enraptured with you, Rose Trelawney, with your bumps and bruises. And home improvements," he added pointedly.

"How unjust! You know Annie said . . ."

"Yes, and I know as well Annie has not been in the attics for a decade, and hasn't noticed whether the Saloon has a carpet or not for the same length of time."

"You must own it is past time that antique was lifted."

"It is very kind of you to take such an interest in us. I fully expect I will see a new mulberry jacket hanging in my closet for the New Year's party. This one I wear, it will not have escaped your notice, is not this season's cut."

"No, nor last year's either," I answered very civilly. "I had thought it to be of an age with the carpet."

"I can't discard it. My mama, when she was alive in 1795, used to be very fond of it," he assured me. Quizzing, of course.

"I doubt her fondness would have endured so long as your own. If you have no more insults or jibes, I shall retire now. Run along and say good night to Adeline. She worries if I am too late."

"You remember what I said, Rose?" he reminded me. "You have not worn out your welcome at Granhurst yet. We don't want you to vanish on us before you have redone the dining room."

He smiled in an attempt to dilute my worries, which served rather to heighten them. "Good night," I said.

"Good night, Rose."

Chapter Nine

I had a good deal to worry me as I lay in bed that night. I had never supposed for more than five minutes I was actually Miss Grafton. I could bear not being a great heiress, and of course was relieved to learn I was not a hired companion. But *who on earth was I*? I felt at home enough here at Granhurst, with servants to do my bidding. Ordering them about came naturally to me, which augured my being accustomed to having them. But at times little things occurred to me—mere details really, but details that spoke of a different sort of life. The house was somewhat disorganized due to its having no real mistress, only Annie and Abigail. Dusty chambers and outmoded curtains also seemed natural to me. 'When money is less tight,' I would think, as natural as breathing, 'they will be changed.' But money was not tight at Granhurst. How did I know so surely that if the Green Saloon were fixed up it would give a good impression, make any callers less suspicious of the state of the rest of the house? Why was I surprised to see Abigail wore better underwear and nighties than day dresses? My own choice would have been to keep up a good appearance. This seemed almost a fixation with me, giving an *appearance* of affluence, and that must surely be a concern of one who is uncertain of her place in society.

This was really only a minor concern; of greater worry was my relationship with Sir Ludwig. I was using him, manipulating him, and knew it. Knew perfectly well that if I smiled prettily and joked him, he would give me whatever I wanted. Yes, I was intimately acquainted with the tricks of getting what I wanted from a man who admired me. Was not this the carrying on of a common lightskirt? Taking money from him for my little luxuries and vanities was second nature to me. I was an adept at it, no beginner. The awful idea was taking hold that I was nothing other than a lady of pleasure. It explained too my showing up under such odd circumstances, and no one raising any hue and cry over my disappearance. I had been kicked out by my latest patron, put back on the streets in the gown in which I had come to him, but wearing beneath some of my acquired finery. Even my knowledge of the world might be explained in this manner. A follower of the drum, trailing her skirts across Europe looking for greener pastures. When my luck was up, I had servants and a good home, when it was down I tried to keep up appearances for the sake of attracting a new patron.

All this was damning enough to keep me awake past midnight, but there was worse knowledge waiting to condemn me. Knowledge of so intimate and personal a nature I hardly know how to put it into words. I was no stranger to physical desire. I felt a rising interest in Sir Ludwig that was surely never felt by a maiden. I wanted him, and knew he felt the same. I knew what was in his mind when he cast those surreptitious glances at me, and was excited rather than frightened as I ought to be, if I were a real lady. Marriage could account for this, perhaps, but I wore no wedding ring.

Was I no better than I should be, then? What a euphemism! A good deal *worse* than I should be, and at such pains to give the impression I was an innocent miss. But surely I was being hard on myself. It was all conjecture after all. I turned resolutely over and commanded sleep to come.

In the morning, it was back to the French lessons for myself and Abbie. Life was to go on as much like normal as was possible in such upset times. Sir Ludwig, we knew, was going into Wickey to see what he could discover of the mysterious man from Bath. (My last patron, come back to reclaim me?) He discovered so little as to be hardly worth the trip. The caller, according to Mulliner, had been a middle-aged man of neat but plain appearance, of middle size and height, with graying-brown hair and driving a hired carriage. He had been well-spoken without giving any air of being scholarly or educated to an outstanding degree. No squint, mole or deformity to pinpoint such a nondescript person any more exactly.

"That description would fit a million men in England," Sir Ludwig said, dissatisfied. "Mr. Gwynne or Morley, for instance, though we know it was neither of them. It also fits Mr. Uxbridge, incidentally. I had Mrs. Lantry give me a rundown on his appearance. He had no distinguishing characteristic whatsoever. 'Not a fellow that would ever stand out in a crowd' was the way she summed him up."

"Did Morley say he would notify the police about Mr. Uxbridge's part in the affair?" I asked him.

"Certainly. He had already been in touch with the local constable, and had spoken to Bow Street a couple of weeks ago, when his niece disappeared. They are trying to find the girl, but doing it quietly in accordance with Morley's wishes. We must be in touch with them as well, I think."

London was a long eighty-five miles away, with unpleasant weather and the roads far from good in this season. I felt guilty indeed to be putting Sir Ludwig to so much trouble on my behalf. I had felt an instinctive dread of advertising in papers, but getting the police to work in private was acceptable to that phantom that ruled my emotions. He was to leave that same afternoon, as making the trip in one day was impossible in this weather.

As things turned out, his trip was unnecessary. Bow Street came to us after luncheon in the body of one Mr. Jethro Williker. Just like Misses Smith, middle-aged men of unobtrusive appearance abounded in our case. Mr. Williker was such an other. His way of expressing himself I would not have described as 'well spoken,' but in other ways he was very average. Kessler spoke first to him, but within a quarter of an hour a message was sent to me to join them. I then knew only that a gentleman had been shown into Sir Ludwig's study, and was on pins and needles to learn if his business had to do with me. My first view of him made me think he was the mysterious gentleman from Bath. I was soon undeceived. I was told his business at once.

"Mr. Williker is from Bow Street, and has some interesting news on Mr. Uxbridge," Ludwig said.

Williker stared into my eyes as though by sheer will power he would make me reveal things unknown even to myself. I was never scrutinized in such a way before or since. All the while he spoke, he stared at me. "He's a charlatan—a confidence man," Williker began. "I was on to his case even before the kidnapping. Lord Nevins set me on to him, became suspicious of Uxbridge, he did. Sold him a painting at a very good price, a Memling it was, which he *said* he was selling for a client. Lord Nevins, he thought nothing of it; then, when the fellow turned up on his step three weeks later with another painting, he became suspicious. That's when he came to us, to see if we knew anything about said paintings. Well sir, I won't conceal the fact we didn't know a thing about them. I'm not what you'd call a connesoor myself, but I know how to conduct an investigation as well as any and better than most. The

Royal Academy I went to direct, and sought an interview with Mr. Benjamin West himself, and was granted same very condescendingly, I might add. Them works, he told me, quick as winking, come from the collection of the late Sir Rodney Grafton, which information I took direct back to Lord Nevins. 'Well, I never heard the Grafton collection was up for grabs,' says his lordship. Nor was it. Our first thought was that Uxbridge had stolen the paintings outright, but the executor, a Mr. Morley, he said it was no such a thing. Mr. Uxbridge was a sort of adviser. Nothing a body could do about that, but that wasn't the end of Mr. Uxbridge's story."

He settled back in his chair comfortably and went on. "If he'd kept to selling the real and authentic goods he'd have got clean away with it—clean away, but what did the fellow do but try to palm off a forgery on Sir Geoffrey Carlisle, who knows more about pictures than you and me and Michelangelo put together. A Georgieown it was, Italian painter. A very sly way he set about it. He *showed* him one picture which was the real goods, then took it away while Sir Geoffrey made up his mind, and delivered a fake. Carlisle threatened to have in the law, and our friend Uxbridge raises his hands and says it's all a terrible mistake. He's brought the wrong picture, a copy that had been made up, and promptly trots back with the original. Then doesn't he turn around, Uxbridge, and try to sell the copy to another chap, who as luck would have it knew of Sir Geoffrey's recent purchase. Well sir, the fat was in the fire then. A warrant was sworn out for his arrest and my investigation turned up some pretty smelly deals."

"When did all this happen?" Ludwig asked.

"Started as early as September when the first picture was taken to Lord Nevins, but Uxbridge's career goes back a long ways beyond that. His usual way of proceeding is to get himself on the right side of a party with a good bit of artworks he doesn't know the value of, and insinuate himself into confidence. Usually by offering to buy some small piece, then bit by bit he gets to taking over, stringing the cove along he can get him a very good price for the works, which he sells off at a fair price, giving the owner a part of what he gets. Widows and such like are his usual dupes. It was the business of the forgery that did him in. As long ago as December 4 I made a trip to Shaftesbury to deal with Mr. Uxbridge, but his housekeeper told me he was in London. Very well, says I to myself, I'll pick him up in London, but neither hide nor hair of him did I find. Then on the sixth we got the letter from Mr. Morley about his niece being gone, and I began wondering if there wasn't some connection between the two things."

"How did you come to end up here at Granhurst?" Sir Ludwig managed to slip in when he stopped for breath.

"I was over to Shaftesbury yesterday again looking for Mr. Uxbridge, and find he's broken up housekeeping. The old malkin at the door wasn't the same housekeeper he had before, which made me suspect something amiss. I stuck around and got in after dark by means sometimes employed in my trade, to find him gone for good. All his personal effects taken away, so I doubt he means to return. There wasn't so much as a shoe in the closet, nor a shirt in the drawers."

I saw Sir Ludwig's mind was working. He too had been there yesterday, but as it was his first visit, he had assumed the housekeeper was Mr. Uxbridge's regular one. She must have been paid to keep quiet I suppose. I had little time to think of it as Williker was off again, and I didn't mean to miss a word.

"I learned in the village Uxbridge regularly employs a couple called the Dobbles, a rough and ready pair they are by all accounts, as popular as smallpox. I figure the affair with Sir Geoffrey tipped him the clue he was hot, and Mr. Morley tells me as well there was a woman at his place asking pretty hard questions. With one thing and another, he's tipped us the double. Flown the coop, as you might say. Morley told me yesterday evening of your visit, and I thought I'd stop to have a word with yourself on my way back to London. The housekeeper there tells me you were mighty interested in this Miss Smith woman." It was Sir Ludwig's turn to have his soul burned by the gimlet eyes of Mr. Williker.

He outlined my history, which I think was no revelation to Williker, as he nodded in a way that indicated he had heard it all before. "It's a rum set-up surely, such a brace of Misses Smith and people dabbling in the arts, and vanishing under our noses. All part and parcel of the Grafton case when we get to the bottom of it," he told us.

"If we ever do," I said wearily.

"Never you fret your head about that, miss. I haven't but one unsolved case in my files, and that one never will be solved, for it's Lord . . . it's a lord that stole the necklace, and those lads stick together worse than gypsies."

"I don't see how we will solve it unless we get a line on Uxbridge," Sir Ludwig mentioned.

"Aye, he's the bird at the bottom of it sure as I'm a *homo sapiens*, but I've a fair notion where he's to be found right enough. Spoke many a time to Mr. Morley about some three-pronged picture he wanted him to buy, and it was a Mrs. Knightsbridge in Scotland that had one corner of it. Morley had another. A regular ugly thing it was. Beats old Nick why anyone would want it, but it was old you see, and age is a wonderful thing in art. The older it is, the better the collectors like it. I investigated Mrs. Knightsbridge, and she's his sort of a victim. A rich woman left a bunch of pictures by some relatives, and handling the whole herself. I wouldn't be surprised to hear our Mr. Uxbridge has nipped up to Edinburgh to try his luck with her."

I sat, trying to catch Sir Ludwig's eye when this familiar name and locale arose. He steadfastly refused to look at me, thus giving me absolutely no clue as to whether we were to mention our knowledge of the woman. Why did I feel that spurt of dislike of her every time I heard her name?

"It is Mrs. Knightsbridge who was Miss Smith's last

117

employer. Did Morley happen to mention that to you?" Kessler decided to ask.

"Aye, so he did. The suspicion arises as to whether Miss Smith wasn't a cohort of Mr. Uxbridge's, of course. In former times he worked alone, but it is certainly possible he took up with Miss Smith at some point, and got her to come along to Grafton's. I can't think why he'd do it, when the woman was held in such almighty high esteem by Mrs. Knightsbridge. Seems to me the woman would have been easy plucking between the two of them. But happen he wanted to milch a few more pictures from Grafton before heading up north. Don't see why he'd have Miss Smith come down, but then in affairs of the heart the head will ofttimes be overruled. They say she was a fair-looking woman, Miss Smith."

"Do you consider him a dangerous man? I mean, would he be likely to kill Miss Grafton?" Kessler asked.

"Kidnapping and killing haven't been his way till the present. Still, a fellow as would steal can't have an overpowering conscience, and if the rewards were great enough, I fancy he'd turn his hand to kidnapping or murder without too much hesitation. Or if the danger were great enough, for he don't actually stand to make anything out of kidnapping the girl as he hasn't demanded a ransom. She must have caught him dead to rights, poor girl."

Mr. Williker then turned his attention to me, giving me a severe catechism regarding all my recent history. I answered him as well as I could. He nodded, then mentioned, "I believe I saw you out in the parks yesterday on my way to Shaftesbury. I heard your story in Wickey, and took the opportunity to have a look around the place. Idle curiosity you might say."

"Was it you who hit me?" I asked.

"Eh?" he asked, completely stunned.

He was enchanted with my story. This at least was a new bit of information for him. He assured me he had not descended from his gig. Had done no more than drive up to the door, turn around and proceed to Shaftesbury. He had planned to stop off here today even without hearing from Morley that Sir Ludwig had been there yesterday, on the off chance that my turning up on December the second might hold some key in the Grafton case.

"So someone is after you, too," he said, with a considering frown on his face. "That surprises me," he confessed. It hurt him to have to admit it. He looked physically pained. He ran over the pertinent points a few more times, ending up by turning an accusing eye on me and saying, "I do believe I was wrong about you. I can't see you're necessary in the case at all. You don't belong. I wonder if you're not a red herring." I waited for him to proclaim me a scarlet woman as well, but I wore the navy bombazine and looked respectable that day.

Sir Ludwig's eyes flickered to me, and his lips were unsteady. Mr. Williker was aware of no opprobrium in the description. It was all business with him. "Yes sir, you're not in the case at all. It could be all coincidence. Oh, I see you shaking your head at me, Sir Ludwig, but the fact of the matter is coincidence is an amazing creature. I had a case over in Devonshire where no less than *three* ladies had sapphire rings they couldn't account for, all close enough alike to be the one was lifted from a vault. Coincidence!" he said, lifting his shoulders and indicting me with the word.

I had the distinct sensation I had been pushed well to the rear of his mind. Not forgotten, he was too much the bulldog for that, but shunted aside.

"What do you plan to do then?" Kessler inquired.

"It'll be a jaunter up north for me. Bad time of the year for it, but then no time of the year is the right time for such a trip. Dr. Johnson, Dr. Samuel Johnson I mean, had the right saying for it. 'The best road a Scotsman will ever see is the road south.' "

"We would appreciate hearing what you learn there," Kessler told him.

"We'll keep in touch certainly. I'd appreciate your letting me know if you solve the young lady's riddle as well," Williker replied, quite clearly implying my fate was in no way interwoven with his case.

"Have you any suggestions as to how we might solve it?" Ludwig asked.

"Best to let the runners handle it," he was told with a touch of professional condescension. "However, as you ask, I would suggest you keep a sharp eye on the little lady. There's some mystery to do with her. I'll take a look into it when I get back from Scotland, if you haven't got it sorted out for yourself by then," he offered just before leaving.

When he was gone, we sat looking at each other rather stupidly. "I wonder if he's right and I am no more than a red herring in all this serious business. Nothing else but a runaway governess who has lost her memory." Of course I mentioned nothing about my other possible identity.

"Who would be bothered skulking in my garden to tap a runaway governess on the head?" he pointed out reasonably. "No, Rose, it's possible you have no corner in the Grafton business. I don't believe it myself, but you're no runaway governess. I'll bet my boots on that. Williker is right about one thing. There's not much we can do. We'll just have to sit tight and wait to hear how he makes out in Scotland. And of course keep a sharp eye on our red herring. Meanwhile, as you dislike the notion of advertising we shall amuse ourselves here in the interim with our New Year's party, and tearing the Saloon to pieces for refurbishing."

And that, with one little exception, is exactly what we did.

Chapter Ten

The exception in our routine was as follows. The next morning I received a note from Miss Wickey asking me to drop in to see her next time I was in the village. There seemed no urgency to it, and I thought little of it, but that there was another enclosure in the envelope. It had been sent out by Mulliner's footboy, who did not await a reply. The note said: "Miss Smith: I am most eager to discuss with you our unfinished business. I shall be at the inn till noon, and expect to see you there, alone. For your own convenience, I know you would prefer it thus. Sincerely, Mr. Smith." That's all. I read it through a couple of times, with my hand trembling. It sounded perfectly menacing, yet as I reread it, there was nothing worse mentioned than 'unfinished business' which could be innocent. And why should innocence require no observers? *I* would prefer that we meet alone. It was impossible not to wonder if Mr. Smith were my last patron. Lover, in other words. If this were the case, he was correct in thinking I would prefer to meet him alone. Yet someone had undertaken to strike me on the head, and if not Mr. Smith, who else? If this was the manner in which Mr. Smith behaved when we were alone, I understood very well why I had fled him, and knew as well I would not meet him alone. My wish was not to meet him at all, but my curiosity had something to say in the matter. Folly to ignore the note altogether. To crumple it up and burn it, as darted into my head. I think all the same I might have done just that if Sir Ludwig had not strolled into the hallway to see who had come to the door. He took one look at my stricken face, then lifted my note from my fingers.

"Let's go," he said.

"He mentions my going alone," I pointed out.

"He says you might prefer to go alone. Do you, in sight of your last meeting with Mr. Smith?"

"No, of course not," I answered. Oh, but I didn't want *him* to go with me!

There was no getting out of it. My bonnet was squashed on my head and my cape flung over my shoulders while I stood thinking of ways of being rid of him, and before I knew what to do, we were off. I haven't a single idea what he said along the way. I have some vague recollection of his never being still a moment, prattling on excitedly about what the 'unfinished business' might be, in a perfectly cheerful way. When we got to the inn, Sir Ludwig went in and made enquiries, but there was no Mr. Smith registered, no message left for me.

He came out, hunched his shoulders and raised his brows. "A hoax," he said. "No, hardly that I suppose. Mr. Smith didn't wish to show his face when he saw you came accompanied. Another effort to get at you, in other words. I hope this makes you realize, Rose, that this is a serious business. The man means to harm you, or kidnap you. A good thing you didn't go jauntering off to that inn alone. Be sure to let me know if he gets any more messages to you. What should we do now? I wonder if there's any point poking around town, trying to find him?"

"Let's go home," I said. If Mr. Smith were at all eager to recover me, he'd find a way. I can't say I was eager to return to a nondescript gentleman with a nasty habit of striking me. We were half way back to Granhurst before I remembered Miss Wickey's note, and mentioned it.

"Too bad," he said. "I'll ask her who gave her the note to include with hers, but I'll take you home first. You look like the very devil."

"Thank you."

"Peaky is what I mean."

He didn't bother stabling the carriage, but left me at the door and returned straight to the village. Miss Wickey was no help. The note had been shoved under her door, with another note requesting that it be delivered to me. She hadn't read it, of course, my note, but knowing my anxiety to discover who I was, had it sent off to me directly, and merely asked me to drop by and see her when I was in the village, as she often thought of me. It was a dead end, but it did serve to make me realize *someone* knew who I was, and was eager to speak with me. How aggravating to know the answer to my riddle was within five miles of me, and couldn't be reached. I could only sit and wait for another message, but in the ensuing days, none came.

I redeemed some shred of decency in my own eyes very soon. Any slight resemblance to a governess I had previously borne was completely vanished. I behaved and was treated more like the mistress of the place, and a fairly demanding mistress I was, too. I don't know how a party was managed at Granhurst in other years when I was not there to oversee it. This year it was left entirely in my hands. Or would it be more correct to say my hands grasped out and seized the opportunity? At least they were capable hands. Surely no mere mistress knew so well how to execute a polite party. This gave me some slight hope for my character.

After a good deal of rummaging through drawers,

Abbie turned up a list two years old which we used as a basis for this year's list. She helped me direct the cards, but in such an unformed hand that I surreptitiously re-wrote hers when she was out of the room. My own penmanship was good, a trifle overly florid perhaps, with dainty loops and swirls, but a *lady's* hand, not a streetwalker's. 'Artistic,' Abbie called it, while Annie was kind enough to say it was 'illegible,' and she would teach me to write as I had forgotten. The chore had a keen sense of familiarity to it. I felt I had addressed many such a card in times gone by. Almost I could see myself at a desk with a stack of gold-edged cards by me, but no matter how hard I tried to discover what name was on the card as sender, it evaded me. I was happy for such a respectable memory all the same.

Refreshments, decorations, everything but the musicians was left to me. Abbie blinked her eyes in delighted astonishment when I mentioned champagne and lobster patties, and a host of other delicacies, whose names fell from my lips unbidden. Orgeat and fruit punch were banned as beneath us. This was how a party was managed; I knew no other way, but I seemed to know this lavish way very well. Redeemed to respectability by my knowledge of a polite party, I blossomed. If I felt a liking for Sir Ludwig, it was hardly a new thing in the world after all, a mutual attraction between the sexes. Sir Ludwig remained docile throughout, by judicious doses of the indecent bordeaux gown. He was so embarrassed to be caught ogling my bosoms one evening that I even got permission to remove a particularly revolting glass cage of stuffed animals from a corner of the entrance hall and replace it on the table with a very nice Sèvres vase from an upstairs room. Two squirrels and a badger I believe the animals were, with a stuffed owl on a tree branch staring at them with huge glass eyes. Annie claimed the thing for her over-crowded chamber. It was as much as your life was worth to enter that room of hers. Stuffed to the rafters with all manner of junk, not one piece of which was allowed to be even moved, much less thrown out.

I knew how much food and wine was required for the party of one hundred guests, knew we would require extra help from the village, and all the spare pots and pans scoured up for duty, ordered without hesitation the hay for the stables. I had the spare rooms turned out and aired, oversaw the polishing of the lovely crystal chandeliers in the ballroom. The rags came away *brown*; the chandeliers could not have been properly cleaned in two years. I was in my element getting at last a shine on the fine furnishings that had been allowed to dull through indifference. The smell of beeswax and turpentine hung on the air, bringing peace and satisfaction to me. I had been wanting to have an excuse for this clean-up since my arrival.

I was not encouraged to go about outside the house, but guarded by the whole family, I did make the trip to Wickey for the ordering of the curtain material very early in the week, and to see that they didn't order up another salmon-pink carpet with wine roses. I talked Annie out of peach draperies by telling her quietly aside that if she insisted on pink, Sir Ludwig would dig in his heels and buy green again. She soon found herself enraptured with a much prettier shade of dusky rose. The carpet had to be ordered from a London catalogue. Wickey did not every day have an order for an Aubusson carpet. Abbie, bless her soul, fell in love with an elegant carpet of Aubusson design, an ivory ground wrought with deep blue pattern. A very few hints made Sir Ludwig aware how ill these new fineries would suit his ugly green plush sofas. He agreed to let us make the choice of new covering, in his eagerness to get out of the shop. I'm sure we could have gotten permission to rehang every window in the house, for he was champing at the bit to leave. He just said 'Yes' and 'That's fine' to everything, with hardly a glance at it, or the price ticket, either. A little haggling would certainly have lowered the price on such a quantity of items. We 'accidentally' ordered sufficient extra material to cover a few cushions while we were about it.

The house was inundated with noisy and uncouth workmen the next few days. We spent the week sitting on hardbacked chairs while the sofas were out being recovered, but were so busy stitching up the cushions and rooting through the treasure trove of an attic that we hadn't much time to complain. Sir Ludwig found plenty of time to do it for us. He was the sort of a gentleman who was happier with the shabby familiar objects than having his peace disturbed with strangers coming and going in his home. I wondered, every time I saw him take a deep breath and frown when the bell rang how he had adjusted so quickly to *my* troublesome presence.

Annie was quite simply delighted with the whole affair. She was like a child having her first birthday party. Every inch of leftover material of any shape or color was squirreled away in her capacious pockets for taking to her room. She held some supernatural communication with the deceased Ruth Kessler during which she was told to watch out for me. I believe this idea actually insinuated itself into her poor disordered head because Sir Ludwig had developed the habit of enquiring where I was every time I was out of the room for so much as a minute. I learned of this by remarking that every time I entered, one or the other of the family would say, "Ah, here she is now. Safe and sound, you see," or something of the sort. It became rather a joke between us.

"I plan to step into the hallway and ask Chalmers if the extra hay has arrived," I would explain with great gravity to the family. "If I am not back within five minutes, pray be in touch with Bow Street. You will notice that when last seen I was wearing navy bombazine." Naturally I could not every day wear the bordeaux, and in fact it was feeling a shade tighter than when it was delivered. It must have been due to the lack of taking exercise, for I strenuously resisted any second helping of anything. I had induced both Abbie and

Ludwig to do likewise, which I considered a great victory. Abbie in particular was making giant strides in her diet. She had a very definite waistline now, of which she was proud. By the ruse of trying new dishes for the party, I got a few ragoûts onto the table, which perhaps helped to account for the taking of no seconds. They were not just as a ragoût should be, somehow.

I suggested a wide ribbon round the waist of Abbie's ballgown to show off her figure, which caused Sir Ludwig to look at me with a start. "What do *you* plan to wear?" he asked. "You don't have a sleeveless gown, and will want to be in gooseflesh like the others."

This detail had not slipped my mind by any means. I had been into the attics with Annie and got out a rather pretty bronze taffeta gown of some obese ancestor, which I had stripped of all flowers and flounces and recut to wear as an underdress. Its lumpy seams would be concealed by a gauzy covering I had under construction. I explained all this to Abbie, and was surprised to see that Sir Ludwig was incensed at the idea.

"It won't cost you a penny," I quizzed him. "As I am already into my salary to the tune of twenty-five pounds, I could not like to run up any higher a bill. Then too my close incarceration here at Granhurst makes a run into town quite impossible. Of course I realize I shall have two or three shillings tacked on to my account, but really, you know, used clothing generally goes for a song."

"It will not be necessary for a guest under my roof to appear at a ball in a gown twenty years old," he said. "Having already cost me close to a thousand with carpets and draperies, I am willing to advance another one or two for materials."

"*Now* he tells me, when he is certain there isn't time to have it made up," I said in a loud aside to Abbie.

Imagine my astonishment when the next day I was handed about twenty pounds of *ghastly* moss green satin, and told I would be taken that same afternoon to Wickey to be fitted by the modiste there.

"Lord, what an ugly color!" Annie said, regarding it.

Sir Ludwig looked at me questioningly. I was in total agreement with Annie, and think some traces of my feelings must have been on my face. "I thought you liked green," he said. "Your first choice was green, if you recall, and you have said a dozen times you dislike the wine gown."

"It's—it's lovely," I exclaimed, trying very hard not to laugh, for he thought he was doing me a great favor. "But there is not time to have it made up before the party. Only two days away now."

"I have spoken to the modiste in the village. She will have it done on time," he pointed out.

"Oh! But really the other one she made me did not fit at all well. I shouldn't like to go to her again," I prevaricated hastily.

"It fit perfectly!" he objected.

Abigail had taken possession of the green satin, and was holding it up to me, frowning. "Stick to your ancient taffeta," she advised bluntly.

"I'm sure they will take it back in the village, for the bolts are uncut, both of them." Good God, and five ells on each, enough to outfit the whole family in moss green satin.

"We'll go back in the morning and you can choose some color that is more pleasing to you," he informed me.

"The bronze taffeta pleases me very well," I answered quickly. I had sufficient duties involving the party that a trip to Wickey at this time would be nothing but an inconvenience, nor was I particularly eager for the villagers to see me flaunting myself in too high a style at Sir Ludwig's expense. "If you want to ensure my appearance doing you credit, however, you might see if you can exchange all this satin for about three yards of dark green velvet ribbon—quarter of an inch, and *dark* green," I emphasized, to ensure not ending up with great whopping bright green bows weighing down my gauze overdress.

He was looking offended, and this must be talked away, for it was this evening I had selected for the time when I would get the paintings in the Saloon changed. Both the Stubbs horses and Gainsborough animals were grating on my nerves, surrounded as they now were by so much elegance. To this end I set aside the material and began a series of judicious compliments on the Saloon. "So charming, so elegant," I said, prior to introducing the ineligibility of horses decorating the walls. "Very modish, don't you think, Sir Ludwig?"

"I like it very much. And it is saved from being overly dainty by the paintings," he added with a challenging eye towards me.

"Ah, the paintings! Yes, I remember we discussed replacing Stubbs' work—how *very well* they would suit your games-room! That pair of Fragonards in your mama's sitting room . . ."

"Ruth would miss them," he replied, unblushing.

"From what one hears of Ruth, I am sure she would gladly give them over to the Saloon. Annie tells me she was a great one for rearranging, and I doubt she intended things to remain static when she died."

"You can hardly say things are *static* when you have changed every stick and rag in the room!" he pointed out.

"Nothing is changed except the Kent commode and rug and curtains," I parried, rather glossing over a few chairs and tables that had found a new home.

"Nothing is the same."

"You said you liked it," I reminded him, far from relinquishing my goal, but discovering it to be more difficult that I had hoped. And I wasn't wearing my bordeaux gown, either.

"I do like it, and I like the horses, too."

"Would you not enjoy to have them in your study, where you spend so much time toting up my bill?" I asked, hoping to cajole him into humor.

"Maybe *one* of them," he thought, "and we could change it for the stag in the study."

"Oh, worse than ever! You cannot be so obtuse as to think those animals do justice to your Saloon!" I cried, outraged to consider a good painting of a horse was to be replaced by a very inferior etching of a stag.

"Do be reasonable, Lud," Abbie said, laughing.

"I have been reasonable, which is not to say I haven't a mind and taste of my own. The horses stay," he decreed, and marched off to his study.

I knew he would not stay away long, however, and sat devising schemes to get him to change his mind. I was afraid he'd have the stag etching in his hands when he returned, but they were empty when he peeped in to see I was present and accounted for. "Still here," I told him with a wave and a smile. I suggested a game of cards, hoping to win at gambling what I had failed to achieve by smiles and persuasion.

"Not tonight," he answered, with a significant glance to his blasted horses. "Why don't you play something for us, Abbie?"

Abbie, as eager as myself to conciliate him, for time was running very short, went to the pianoforte and played a few selections. I sat trying to envision how vastly improved the room would be with the proper paintings. To me, the paintings in any room were always the icing on the cake, and I dislike a cake with poor icing very much. It seemed a great pity all the work and expense was to be ruined by one man's stubbornness. I suppose my eyes were frequently on the walls during the recital, for after a quarter of an hour, I was told bluntly by my host (right in the middle of a waltz) it was petty-minded of me to sulk, when I had had all my own way thus far. "After all, it *is my* home, and I think my taste ought to be represented at least."

How odious it is to be put firmly in the wrong. I had taken upon myself to redo his Saloon to my taste with his money, and was pouting because he wished to have these few small tokens of his execrable taste to remind him he was master *chez lui*. "You're right," I admitted in a peevish mood, "and it is a pity your taste is so very bad."

"Indeed!" he said stiffly, pokering up like an offended dowager.

"And furthermore, the straw rug in your morning parlor is hideous!" I said in a fit of pique, then left the room before he should beat me to it. It was not my plan to stay away. I went no farther than the library to recover my temper and my manners. It was badly done of me to have been so forward and unappreciative of his improvements. I intended to render an apology in some oblique manner before retiring, hoping this unusual circumstance might bring him to change his mind. Before I had quite recovered, however, he appeared at the door. My first gratifying thought was that he had followed me, and my hopes soared, but it was not the case. The Kesslers were none of them great readers except for the papers and magazines, but he had come for a book. It was ironic that in this Germanic household there should be such poor representation of the invention of Gutenberg. There was the library to be sure, with several shelves bearing dusty tomes, but nothing of a light, poetic or romantic nature. Nothing a body would actually be tempted to read, in either English or French. Even Voltaire and Rousseau were missing. Descartes, dating from the seventeenth century, was the most modern French writer, and the English stopped with a few tattered copies of the *Tattler*.

"Oh, this is where you ran off to to stamp your feet and scream, is it?" he asked, with a lifted brow and an eye not yet empty of anger. "I thought you would be in the morning parlor, tearing up the straw rug."

There was a strong urge to answer this piece of insolence in kind, but I stifled it. "Oh no, I am not that strongly opposed to it."

"That's good, because I have no plans to change it."

"Or the pictures," I added for him.

"Just so," he said over his shoulder, for he had turned his back on me in mid-conversation to examine the books.

"Looking for something to read, are you?" I asked

casually. Had that foolish question been put to me, I would have declared I had come to take a bath, but perhaps he wanted to smooth over the squabble.

"Yes, I like to read a little philosophy before sleeping. I find it soporific."

"That is hardly a compliment to the philosophers!"

"It is not intended as one. Philosophy is arrant nonsense, most of it."

"How can you consider a search for truth and wisdom nonsense? It is the most serious subject in the world."

"Truth and wisdom are not to be found in books, Miss Smith." The 'Miss Smith' informed me I was still in disgrace. "Every man must make the painful discovery for himself. I read it to see where these fellows have run amok."

"To see where Plato and Aristotle and Kant and those other geniuses have gone astray, you mean?"

"That's the idea," he answered blandly. "They were only human, like me."

Ignorance is bad enough; arrogance is worse, but an arrogant ignoramus is intolerable. When he pulled his monocle out of his pocket and rammed it into his eye, I could conciliate no more. "It is incredible that the Teutonic race, which gave us Leibniz, Kant and Schiller should have so far retrogressed as to throw up only a Ludwig Kessler to correct them."

"I was born and bred in England, ma'am, and have never been in Germany in my life." I was only rarely 'ma'am,' at the lowest ebb of our relations or the height of disagreements. I had touched a little nerve then, and was pleased.

"If you were born in a stable it wouldn't make you a cow I suppose," I suggested with a polite yawn.

"Oh, no, a bull, surely."

The best way to deal with that sort of obtuseness is a dignified silence, and I wish I had kept a rein on my tongue. However, he took not the least exception to being called a Bierwurst. I doubt he knew it to be a beer sausage, or maybe he was gratified at having incited me to such a display of bad temper. I'm sure every jot of my considerable wrath was evident on my face. Nothing else would have rung that sardonic smile out of him. He lifted out the monocle. "I can be *led*, Rose, as you well know. I cannot be driven."

"I had a *mule* like that once."

"I once had a bitch with a particularly nasty disposition. I had to get rid of her."

I don't expect you have ever been called a bitch. It exerts an indescribable and in my case uncontrollable fury in the breast. I reached right out and slapped his face, hard. Caught off guard, he was not prepared to stop me. He just looked stunned, as I realized too late what I had done—the enormity of it, and the ill-timing.

"I'm sorry! Ludwig, I didn't mean to . . ." I stopped in mingled horror and embarrassment, trying to read his expression. It was still stunned, but rapidly recovering to anger. My hands reached out involuntarily, and I grabbed his sleeve. He didn't say a word of either vituperation or forgiveness. He regarded me like a man hypnotized for about forty seconds, then he smiled enigmatically and reached his arms out to encircle my waist. I felt such a great wave of relief he wasn't angry that I was a little delayed in responding. Before anything more could come of this promising beginning, there was the sound of running in the hall. Abbie had come to haul us back to the Saloon.

I still wished to apologize, to explain my unpardonable behavior. I later secured about two seconds in which to do it, while Annie toured the room blowing out candles and Abbie poked down the fire, just before we all retired.

"Sir Ludwig," I began, in a voice that sounded unnatural with propriety, even to myself.

"If you are rehearsing to apologize, Rose, don't," he said. "It was inconsiderate of me to goad you when you have so much on your mind."

I had nothing on my mind but the apology. I do not often tender an apology, and for some reason I felt rather cheated. When we steel ourselves to do the right thing, we like to get on and do it. "Anyway, I'm sorry," I said.

"Then I suppose you force me to say, with what sincerity I can find, there is nothing to be sorry for. But if you are standing there with that scowl on your face waiting for *me* to now apologize, you'll have a long wait."

"I only expected you to say I was forgiven." This had an abject sound to it that disgusted me. "That you aren't angry, I mean," I adjusted rapidly.

"I am blazing angry—that Abbie interrupted us," he said with a boyish smile. Then he walked off and took the poker from Abbie, for of course the final poking down of the fire is the peculiar prerogative of males. A mere female cannot be trusted with such an onerous chore unless she has the felicity of living apart from men.

The next morning when I came downstairs, the paintings in the Saloon had been changed. I had found a new way to bearlead a gentleman—by slapping him on the face! Not a word was said about it, but when I went into the Saloon once more to lament this one bone in my throat, the Fragonards, dainty *fête-champêtre* scenes of lovely ladies in flower-bedecked swings being pushed by dashing cavaliers had replaced the horses. Gainsborough's human animals remained. It was not complete capitulation. They were insignificant on a side wall and were not so bad as the horses, in any case. I stood in the center of the room, looking all around and smiling at the wonder I had created. It was a room anyone might be proud of, I thought.

Sir Ludwig entered at the door, looking rather sheepish at his giving in. "I suppose you will now start in on me about the cat and dog," he said.

"No indeed I will not! You deserve one token of your own atrocious taste. There was a snake in Eden, after all," I replied, but in a rallying good-natured way, to

134

show him I appreciated his sense in following my advice. "You must own this is an improvement. Now you have a Saloon to be proud of."

"Fool that I am, I was not ashamed of it before."

"Oh, no, I didn't mean it was bad enough to be ashamed of, but now it is lovely."

"I collect I ought to be thanking you for your help."

"Just bear it in mind when you are adding up my bill. I daresay ten or twenty years from now, when your wife wishes to redo it again, Annie will be scolding her that Rose Trelawney especially wanted to have those Fragonards hung in the Saloon. Pray do not consider the room is to be set under glass, immutable forever." I hoped the word 'wife' might joggle his memory as to his interrupted business in the library the night before, but it failed.

"Do you think then that in ten or twenty years Miss Trelawney will have left us?"

"It begins to look as though she has made herself a life tenant, does it not? I had thought we would have heard from Mr. Williker by now."

"Scotland is a long trip, and the roads at this time of the year are not good. For him to get there and get a letter back to us would take two weeks, or close to it."

It was to be business, but the servant in the hallway took an occasional peep in at us, which might account for his failing to grasp this opportunity.

"I feel I ought to be doing something in the meanwhile to find myself."

"We can insert advertisements in the paper, if you are overcoming your aversion to it."

Strangely enough, I had almost forgotten about my peculiar position. My mind was more bent on claiming the indisputable right to remain on than getting away. Busy with the renovations and the ball, with the excitement of the New Year approaching, I had resolutely pushed all conscious thoughts of my position back to a corner of my mind. It would, of course, intrude when I was alone, particularly at night when I lay in bed, but hard as I would try then to drag forth some pertinent memory or clue, nothing came. I had more dreams, my sleeping hours were more productive than my waking ones. I dreamed again of sheep and highlands, of myself sitting at a desk writing cards, of standing under a sweltering sun in Italy, looking at the Arno, and then painting Abbie as a Botticelli grace. I dreamed once again of the Medici triptych, after a visit from Mr. Gwynne, who dropped by occasionally to talk of art with Sir Ludwig and myself. I had not overcome my aversion to a public advertisement, but began to see I must be ruled by common sense, and was firming up my resolve to do it. "Maybe we should advertise," I said, a little reluctantly.

"Shall we wait to hear from Mr. Williker?" he suggested.

"Very well," I agreed at once, snatching at the delay.

"As to doing anything to discover who you are, outside of advertising I can think of nothing. Bow Street notwithstanding, I feel you must be wound up in the Grafton affair, and if he can run Uxbridge to earth, we'll discover you have some corner in the muddle. So, Red Herring, let it not spoil our party. I am looking forward to our first party, Rose."

Chapter Eleven

Christmas was not marred by any intrusion of my past. It was a happy event, celebrated in the customary way. The party for New Year's was marred by a host of sundry annoyances, not least amongst them an echo from my past. Some of the guests arrived a day early, and I saw right away they were not the sort to merit champagne, nor the huge housecleaning we had undertaken. They were inelegant county people who would have been quite satisfied with the normal fare of Granhurst. I was introduced to two persons already familiar to me by anecdote. Valerie Hodgkins, the late Kessler's first love was there, a dumpy woman whom it was difficult to imagine any man having loved, ever. Annie assured me well within the woman's hearing, "She was not so Friday-faced when she was eighteen, nor so chubby." The woman did not appear to recognize the satinwood commode; she scarcely glanced at it. Nor was there any tarnished tea pot in the kitchen; I had been down to check. The other lady was the one Annie had castigated as muffin-faced, a former flirt of Sir Ludwig. She was not quite so ugly as Valerie, though I would have called her fubsy-faced myself. A squashed, fat face, with a figure to match. She was nudging thirty, still single, and still determined to try her hand at landing Kessler. He was surprisingly dexterous in avoiding her. He must have kept a sharp eye in her direction to move off every time she advanced towards him, and to do it always so nonchalantly that it could not be said he was running.

I was the object of much interest to all these relatives, who suggested variously that I was a French spy, an actress and a fortune hunter, though it was all done by innuendo of course, and in a perfectly forgiving way. It was Fubsy-face's mother who insinuated the last-named charge. "How very odd you turned up at the door of a bachelor's establishment," she said, regarding me with a knowing look.

"Yes, though to be fair, Mrs. Veeley, I had no notion the Reverend Mulliner was a bachelor when I went there," I answered, refusing to understand her significant glances to Sir Ludwig.

"Mulliner? Good gracious, were you there, too? Another bachelor! I hadn't heard you had tried a hand with him. But you came to Ludwig, instead."

"Yes," I answered civilly, "for it was commonly said in Wickey that he was much richer."

She bridled up and looked sharply to her daughter, who looked at Sir Ludwig with a warning glance. "Is the engagement to be announced at the ball then?" Mrs. Veeley asked him in a heavy-handed attempt at irony, while Fubsy-face smirked.

"Why, no, we think it more proper to discover Miss Trelawney's real name first," Sir Ludwig replied, impassive as a rock to all the jibes.

"What are you doing to discover it?" the mother asked.

"We are making investigations," he answered vaguely. "Ah, Rose, would you mind coming with me to meet the Helterns, who are just arriving?" he asked, offering his arm and smiling politely as we walked away.

"You see how useful I am in guarding you from Miss Veeley," I quizzed him. "I've noticed you darting off like a frightened hare every time she advances on you. This should be taken into consideration when you bill me for draperies and gowns."

"I'll add it on to your marriage settlement," he answered. "I suppose I must make some provision for you as you are a fortune-hunting pauper."

I was presented to the Helterns, who were as dowdy as all the rest, and viewed me with as much distrust. I was the freak again, the exotic bird to be examined for plumage and habits.

"What a charming party it promises to be after all," Sir Ludwig said after he had turned the new guests over to the butler. "Do you not take the feeling you ought really to be behind bars?"

"It is an excellent idea. I feel a strong urge to bite. The Trelawney is possessed of a highly unstable temperament, you must know."

"I come to understand why. I even understand why the Trelawney nearly bit my head off when first I met her."

I did not bite, except verbally. I must own I gave the Veeleys a few sharp setdowns, and when the son of the Helterns suggested I was welcome to return with him to London, which I would find vastly more amusing that being Ludwig's mistress in the country, I told him quite sharply I doubted London or anywhere would be at all amusing under his patronage. He did not take it in bad part at all, but continued putting his proposition to me at every opportunity.

When the evening of the ball arrived, we were all still on speaking terms. Scarcely a friendly word was exchanged, but we did speak of social nothings. I donned the bronze gown with a little assistance from Abbie, who looked very well in her gown with the satin waistband. I had no jewels, of course.

"Why don't you borrow my topaz eardrops?" she offered.

"I should wear my diamonds with this outfit," I answered heedlessly.

She looked at me, startled. "Do you have *diamonds, Rose?*"

"Good Lord! Whatever possessed me to say such a thing? Wishful thinking, I daresay." Yet it had slipped out so naturally—'my diamonds.' I had quite a clear picture of one particular set of diamonds in my mind, too. Not large, but well-matched, a necklace and bracelet and earrings. I could almost feel the lobes of my ears tingle. *They were always uncomfortable,* flashed into my head.

"Maybe Lud would let you wear mama's diamonds," Abigail suggested, uncertainly.

"No! Don't think of it. What would all your relatives say?"

"Why, more of what they are already saying," she laughed. "I'll get the topazes."

They added at least a little sparkle to my ensemble. When Ludwig gave me a careful perusal, however, I wished more strongly than ever that I were wearing someone's diamonds.

"One would never take it for second-hand," he complimented mildly. I could see right away he didn't like the outfit.

"Your jacket isn't showing its twenty-odd years, either," I returned. It did look two or three years old though, and was added to my list of items in that house to be replaced.

"I should have thought to lend you some jewelry," he mentioned, still regarding my gown without enthusiasm.

I don't think this was actually the improvement he had in mind. The gauze overdress was designed to conceal, and it filled its function pretty well. With the likes of the McCurdles coming to our party, I was determined to appear in a respectable light. It was partly for this reason I coerced him into opening the ball with Miss Veeley. Partly, too, it was done to restore that pair of female pests to good humor. It put Ludwig in the boughs, but then he had been amazingly hostile throughout the entire visit, constantly repeating when he was beyond his guests' earshot that this had been a wretched idea, and wondering when were they going home.

Mulliner and his housekeeper arrived a little late. Miss Wickey sought me out, and I told her I was sorry I had not got in to see her lately.

I thought it was only the unaccustomed treat of the ball that had her looking more animated than usual, but she soon disillusioned me. "Surprise!" she said, handing a small packet to me. My next thought was that she was giving me a gift, but she explained quickly. "I found it under the dustskirt of your bed. At the rectory, I mean. I think it must have fallen out of a pocket when I shook out your clothing that night you arrived. You remember, Miss Smith, your cape was wet, and I gave it a shake before putting it away?"

I opened the package to be confronted with a ring. A plain golden band it was. A wedding ring. "It's not mine!" I said, handing it back to her.

"Oh but it must be, my dear. I never saw it before, and you were the only one to have used that room in months. It must be yours."

"No, I never saw it before. It's not mine," I insisted, shoving it back.

"You wouldn't remember, would you?" she asked reasonably. "Try it on. See if it fits."

It fit perfectly, slid on just with a little push over the knuckle, as a ring should. "There! I knew it must be yours," she said, smiling happily.

You may imagine how I felt. I looked at it as though it were an evil charm. It was clearly a wedding ring. It was half an inch wide, and felt more like a manacle than a ring. "Thank you," I said, my voice sounding hollow.

"You're welcome, I'm sure. I always had the notion you were a married woman. You had so much self-confidence, managed Mr. Mulliner so well," she added mischievously. "I never had the nerve to go at him as you did. He still complains about you, calls you an arch wife."

My gown had no pocket, and I carried no evening bag with me, so that the thing remained on my finger, quite effectively ruining my night. The party, so long looked forward to, went on around me, but my thoughts were all taken up with this ring, and the new idea it must present me with. I was a married woman. Somewhere in this country or another I had a husband, possibly even children. How was it possible I could forget them? How was it possible I could wish they did not exist? The only silver lining to this dark cloud, and it was a tarnished lining at best, was that I was rid of any lingering doubt as to being a lady of pleasure. I had learned and practiced my manipulative techniques within the respectability of marriage, making me a lady of principles.

But was the ring necessarily mine? I had always thought the cloak, gown and shoes to be borrowed. The ring must have been in the pocket of the cloak when I put it on. It had been removed (for what possible reason?) by the true owner. Yet it fit me perfectly. Felt at home to a peg on my finger.

Sir Ludwig had the second dance with his sister. I think he did not wish to incite the relatives and neighbors to too much conjecture by distinguishing me in any way. It was not till a waltz was struck up that he came to me.

"Is it permissible for Miss Trelawney to waltz, or has she not made her come-out yet?" he asked.

"You must know married ladies are always allowed to waltz," I answered, glancing to the ring, which he had not noticed as yet.

"What, bagged a husband already, have you? I thought it was no more than a *carte blanche* young Heltern was offering you. Has he been annoying you, by the way?"

"Vastly, but no more than everyone else."

"It's been pretty bad, hasn't it?" he asked with a rueful smile.

"It has been horrid, and I begin to feel I have been attacked unjustly, for it turns out I have been married all the time, and you were never in the least danger from me."

"Is that right?" he asked, looking only amused. "Very poor timing, Rose, to remember Ivor when I am as well as compromised by having you here a month. Nothing but a wedding will restore me to respectability."

"You had better offer for Miss Veeley, then," I informed him in an acidic voice. He looked a question.

"What's that supposed to mean?"

I held up my left hand. "It's mine. Miss Wickey found it in my room. It fell out of my pocket, she thinks."

He blinked twice, without saying a word. Suddenly my wrist was grabbed in a painful hold, and I was being pulled from the ballroom. He didn't stop till we got to his office, where he summarily yanked the ring off, nearly taking the finger with it. "This isn't yours. It's much too tight," he said angrily.

"It fits perfectly," I contradicted. Strangely enough, the stubborn thing went back on more easily than it came off.

He reached out to remove it again, but I closed my fingers over it, repeating in a little more detail the story of its turning up after all this time. "It's not yours," he repeated firmly. He went on to outline that the cloak was definitely not mine, though it did, in fact, fit perfectly. As had the gown. It was only the shoes that were loose. "It belongs to whoever you borrowed the cloak from. That's all," he finished up.

"It fits *me*," I insisted.

"Give it to me." He reached his hand out impatiently. I slid it off and handed it to him. He took it over to the lamp and looked on the inside for an inscription. There was nothing but a 'T' inside, enclosed within a diamond

—the jeweler's mark. This ascertained, he put it in his pocket. "It will only cause talk if you wear it tonight. I'll give it back to you later."

Then we stood looking at each other. Neither of us had anything to say, but there was a great feeling of self-consciousness in the room. What was not said was as speaking as words. *This changes everything* was the feeling. It was a very dismal feeling, indeed.

"Shall we have that waltz?" I asked, with an air of indifference.

"Why not, Miss Trelawney?" he replied. We returned to the ballroom and enjoyed a bittersweet dance, during which neither of us said a word but were minutely aware of the closeness of the other. The first time I had been in his arms for more than a second, and it would in all probability be the last. How good it felt, and how sad.

"We'll talk later," he said when the dance was over, as Mr. Heltern began hastening towards me. Ludwig hadn't even the heart to look angry.

It was an interminable evening. I didn't miss a single dance. Some feeling of doom and damnation was upon me, whose dispersal required me to be gay almost to the point of ill-breeding. In the eyes of the McCurdles I went a good deal beyond that point, I could see. I found myself laughing and flirting with all manner of scarecrows, most of whom seemed very out of place at a polite party, but then they were country relatives, unpolished diamonds, no doubt. When the supper was over—that supper over which I had slaved, at least mentally—when the musicians had gone off home and the last of the guests departed to their bedchambers or their homes, Abigail, Annie and myself and Sir Ludwig stood in the hallway, breathing a weary sigh of relief.

"I'm for bed," Annie said, stifling a yawn.

"You run along too, Abbie. I want to speak to Rose," Kessler said.

She twinkled a tired smile at us and ran up the stairs after her cousin. Servants were cleaning away a welter of glasses and hors d'oeuvres plates in the once green, now blue Saloon. "We'll go to my study," Ludwig said, and I followed him there, wondering what he would say.

He closed the door behind us and drew the ring out of his pocket, looking at it with a face showing much the same cheated feeling I felt myself. I reached out for it, not that I wanted it, to be sure. He took my left hand in his and slid it on the appropriate finger. I had no memory of anyone's having done that before, yet someone probably had, in a church, surrounded by my friends and the clergy. He grabbed my hand impulsively and raised it to his lips. "We don't really *know*, Rose," he said uncertainly.

I was more angry than sorry. How dare fate cheat me out of this moment? He was as well as saying he loved me, wanted to say it I knew, and I was strongly inclined to hear the words, even if I was married, which was very wrong of me, of course.

I proceeded to try to weasel it out of him. "What difference would it make anyway?" I asked, adopting a pout. "The behavior of your relatives towards me has made it perfectly clear . . ."

"Don't be foolish," he scoffed, squeezing my hand quite painfully.

"I suppose you mean me to understand that if it weren't for this ring you would be offering marriage to a stray picked up off the streets."

"No, no, picked up at a rectory—much more respectable."

"I doubt very much I am respectable. I probably ran away from him, whoever he is. Maybe I'm divorced," I mentioned hopefully.

"Maybe you were never married at all. We don't even know the ring came from the cloak—*borrowed* cloak, you wore. We must start advertising at once. It is foolish to have waited so long."

"I see you are eager to be rid of me," I said, trying to goad him into some sort of declaration, however vain the effort.

145

"Rose Trelawney, you are quite shameless," he declared, "and so am I." He swept me into his arms and kissed me more resoundingly than I had intended, and I had planned on more than a peck on the cheek. "Now that is what I would do if I were sure you aren't a married lady," he said, his lips against my ear and his voice unsteady.

Suddenly I was sure, absolutely positive. The ring I had forgotten, but not these sensations stirring within me. I pulled abruptly away, flustered and embarrassed.

"I'm sorry," he said, surprised. "I thought you—expected it."

"I did." Oh but I hadn't expected this sudden onrush of knowledge, this cold certainty that I had every right to the ring I wore. I felt it with the fingers of my right hand, frowning at the sudden memories that washed over me.

"Rose—really there is no reason to assume you are married. There are a dozen possibilities to account for the ring."

"No, it belongs to me."

"You can't know that."

"I *do* know it."

"How the hell can you be so sure of that, when you've forgotten everything else?"

"I don't know, but I'm sure. Good night."

He didn't answer, but remained behind, frowning darkly. I lay awake for hours myself that night, but I didn't hear Sir Ludwig come upstairs.

Chapter Twelve

We were busy the next day with guests departing, and setting the house to rights after the party. I was treated with all the deference owing to a married lady by Sir Ludwig, and as if the ring had never been found by the other two. They looked at it, shrugged their shoulders, and said it might have come from anywhere.

"Imagine the rectory not being cleaned out for a month," was Annie's comment. I didn't say so, but I wondered how many months it had been since the collection of boxes beneath her bed had been disturbed.

"Didn't old Mrs. Wickey, when she was alive, wear a ring like that?" Abbie asked her brother, who heartily supported this spurious memory. As if Miss Wickey wouldn't recognize her own mother's wedding ring! In fact, I believe she wore a gold band on her right hand.

In the late afternoon we prepared an advertisement for the papers and discussed in what cities it ought to be placed. We chose the largest centers in the four corners of the kingdom, along with Edinburgh and Glasgow.

We agreed that before it would reach the papers, be circulated and any enquiries made to us, we might expect a lapse of a couple of weeks. The next day the guests were all gone, leaving behind a sense of letdown. It was back to routine, French in the mornings, painting, reading, music. I finished Abbie's portrait and we had a showing in my studio for the family, honoring the occasion with a bottle of champagne. As I mentioned, Abbie was posed as a nymph in a diaphanous piece of drapery. She stood with a hand on the corner of a Greek statue, the other holding a dove. It turned out rather well. I was pleased with the job. In a gilt frame it might even do for a wall in some not too conspicuous room.

Annie stood with her arms folded regarding it. "Why hasn't she got on some decent clothes? You ought to have worn your ballgown, ninny."

"Don't I look pretty, Lud?" Abbie asked.

"The portrait is beautiful," he decided, regarding it critically.

"I hadn't quite the acres of flesh to work with that your friend Rubens had," I pointed out, trying to get him back into his former mood of jokes and insults.

"Professional, I would say." He looked at me, questioningly. "I wonder if you aren't known as an artist."

But there were no well-known female artists in the kingdom, so I was not likely to find my name by that means, if that was what he had in mind.

Annie began hinting outrageously that I should render her face in oils. What a task! But a challenge—it would be interesting. I ran in my mind over Hogarth's Gin Alley for a likely pose. "I should be happy to, Annie, but you must buy the materials yourself. I don't wish to fall any deeper into debt. I already owe another couple of guineas for the newspaper ads."

"No doubt your husband will be happy to repay the entire debt," he answered, without even a smile. He was being polite to me, damn his eyes.

I outlined the size of canvas I wished, really my sole

requirement as I had a good supply of pigments. As I held out my hands to approximate the width, I noticed him looking at my left hand, to see if I wore the ring. I never put it on, but I often took it out of the drawer when alone and looked at it.

"You don't wear the ring?" he asked later, when Abbie and Annie were off chattering over the portrait.

"No, I don't."

"I'm surprised it isn't mentioned in the village. Miss Wickey must have kept it to herself."

"Ashamed of her housekeeping, I expect," I answered.

"I'm surprised you didn't turn the place out while you were there."

I can't tell you how my heart soared at this speech. It was the first *normal* speech he had made since the night of the party.

"Oh but it *was* cleaned once a month, you see, so I left it alone. It is only when I enter a room as chaotic as in a painting by Jan Steen that I exert myself."

By evening, we were quite back to normal, with a few taunts about the floor covering in the morning parlor on my part, and a mention of the size of my bill on Kessler's. Not a word about a husband happy to pay up for me.

The next morning Sir Ludwig received a letter from Edinburgh. It happened to be myself who took up the mail from the salver in the hall, and I ran straightway to his office to see what J. Williker had to tell us. He held the letter a minute in his hands, hesitating to open it. I think he feared to read what might be enclosed. At last I could control my patience no longer, and seized it to tear it open myself. He read over my shoulder a message that was as confusing as all the rest of this bizarre case.

"Dear Sir Ludwig: Re the matter discussed with you at Granhurst, I have run into an unexpected situation here. Mrs. Knightsbridge is not in Scotland. She left on November 15 for London with friends, and has not been home since. There never was any Miss Smith in her employ. She has for companion a Miss Empey, who accompanied her south. Her secretary, Mr. Soames, tells me he received an unusual request of his employer in late November. She wrote him enclosing a letter to be forwarded to Mr. Morley in Gillingham if she received any letter from him. Mr. Soames did not read the Morley letter."

"How odd!" I said, reading it again to make sure I had it right.

"That's Miss Smith's character reference she was forwarding to Morley," Kessler pointed out. "Must be, the time, just right."

"Why should she give a reference to a person she didn't employ?"

"I don't know. It begins to look as though Mrs. Knightsbridge is in it up to her eyes."

"I never liked her above half. I bet I *knew* her. Could it be *I* am Miss Empey, and hate her because she's my cruel employer, and she was posing as Miss Smith herself? Uxbridge spoke of her to Morley about the triptych. Perhaps she and he are in it together."

"Pity he doesn't mention their ages or appearance. You could very well be Miss Empey, and you're *not* married at all, just as I knew."

I realized his reason for jumping at this straw was no more than an eagerness for me to be unattached. It was very sweet, but not very helpful.

"But why would Mrs. Knightsbridge do such a deceitful thing? She owns a museum—she must be rich," I said, grappling with the tangled skein of the puzzle.

"Maybe *you're* Mrs. Knightsbridge," he mentioned next.

"Maybe I'm Princess Augusta!" I countered. How dare he suggest I was that hateful woman? "What else does he say?"

We read on down the letter.

"Mr. Uxbridge is not here, has not been in touch with Mr. Soames at all. It begins to look as though he and

150

Mrs. Knightsbridge are in on the thing together. I'll be in contact with you as soon as I return south. I leave tomorrow a.m. Your respectful servant, J. Williker."

"Why should he think Uxbridge and Mrs. Knightsbridge are in on it together," I wondered. "If she is Miss Smith, she has created a good deal of mischief for Uxbridge, pointing out the Giorgione forgery."

"I don't know where he gets that idea. As Mrs. Knightsbridge gave false references for Miss Smith, it looks more as if Miss Smith is either herself or this Miss Empey, the pair working together to spike Uxbridge's gun. Which would account for his kidnapping Miss Smith—but what happened to the other lady? She has to be you, Rose. You must be one of them."

"I refuse to be Mrs. Knightsbridge. I don't like her."

"No, you're Miss Empey." He looked very well pleased with this arbitrary interpretation, making me a maiden. Oh, but I wasn't; I was married, and I refused to be Mrs. Knightsbridge!

We read and re-read that letter till I'm sure we both had it by heart, regretting its terseness. We were eager to learn a dozen more details. Why had the two ladies come south? What ages were they, what their appearances? We sat on discussing it for a full hour. I was alternately Miss Empey and Mrs. Knightsbridge, but either way, I was a sneak, giving false references or using them. Why does one pretend to be what one is not but for illegal purposes? Sir Ludwig was inventive in finding ways to whitewash me. He was convinced the wicked Mrs. Knightsbridge was using me, and quite often mentioned blackmail, without, I believe, quite tumbling to it that blackmail is not used against perfectly innocent persons. It might be used against a ruined woman, though, if she were trying to pass herself off as respectable. You may be sure I didn't mention this possibility.

Eventually we proceeded to the next question: What were we to do about it? "Williker should be here in a day or two. We'll wait to see what he has to tell us," Sir Ludwig decided.

I wasn't in a mood for waiting. I wanted to do something, but hardly knew what. In the afternoon, we received a call from Mr. Morley, with a new problem to worry him. He was falling away to a skeleton. "It has arrived!" he announced in a voice of doom.

"What has?" we asked in unison.

"The ransom note," he replied, handing it to Ludwig, who ripped it out of his fingers in alarm. "Good God, it's from Miss Smith!" he exclaimed.

I don't know what thoughts were in Ludwig's mind, but the worst possible things reeled through my own. I was linked up with a kidnapper. Miss Smith—my employer or employee—was a kidnapper, and I was in it up to my neck. I soon had the note from his hands and perused it hastily. "Only ten thousand pounds?" I asked, surprised.

"That is a good deal of money," Sir Ludwig pointed out.

"Oh, yes, but for an heiress of the caliber of Miss Grafton, I would have thought more would be demanded. The estate was worth fifty thousand, I recall."

"I'm glad it was no higher," Morley said. "That sum I can raise very easily. I am on my way to London now. Miss Grafton has ten thousand in the funds, and that can be sold out quickly. Had she demanded more, I would have been obliged to raise a mortgage or sell off some of the collection, and that would take a long while."

I exchanged an understanding glance with Kessler. The kidnapper was well informed of the financial situation of Miss Grafton, then. Knew exactly how much might be demanded and got in a short space of time. Ludwig mentioned this to Morley.

"You mean to imply it is Mr. Uxbridge," he said, "but the fact is Miss Smith knew as well how financial affairs stood. I cannot think Uxbridge would do it. He was a nice fellow. Not quite so bright and knowledgeable about art as I was led to believe. He took too low a sum for some works he sold, but I cannot believe he would sink to this."

"He didn't disappear for no reason," Ludwig reminded him.

"How did Miss Smith come to know about the money?" I queried.

"Mrs. Lantry confessed to me she told her. The woman asked outright, which looks suspicious. They had a long chat about it one day, the day before the kidnapping, it was. It looks as though Miss Smith is our culprit. I must pay. I hope I do the right thing."

"How is the payment to be made?" I asked.

"I will be informed," he answered, still worried. "I will receive another communication. She tells me not to notify the police, and I shan't do it, but as you were so interested in the case, Sir Ludwig, and seem such a sharp fellow, I decided to talk it over with you. I'm not sure I ought to go to London at all at this time."

"I wouldn't think of it. Write to London and have them sell the funds and have the cash on hand when you get the next notice."

"You think I ought to pay, then?"

"You don't have much choice if you want to see your niece alive."

"That was my feeling. I miss having Uxbridge to advise me. One dislikes to do it, but I must. I was wondering—do you think I should demand some proof she is alive and well?"

"Absolutely."

"What sort of a thing should I ask for? I have been fretting about it a good deal. A piece of clothing or hair is no good. That could be taken from a corpse. How could I be sure she is alive?"

"Don't hand over the money till you have seen her— have her back."

"Aye, that would be best, but if they tell me to take the money to some dark, secluded spot, promising to hand her over, and don't do it, where am I? I have

153

thrown away ten thousand pounds that don't belong to me, and still my niece is not back."

"Let me know how it is to be done," Sir Ludwig said at once. "I'll help you."

"Oh that would be monstrous kind of you," he said. I took the idea this was why he had really come. To get someone to handle the exchange for him. Surely he had not planned to go to London at such a time. I felt extremely sorry for the poor man. He at least was above suspicion of being guilty of anything but foolishness and cowardice.

"Where did the note come from? What is the postmark on it?" I asked.

"There is no mark. It had been put under my front door when I came downstairs this morning. Delivered by hand, you see. They cannot be very far away."

I remembered Miss Wickey receiving a note for myself in the same manner. Sir Ludwig looked at the envelope. His brows rose, and an expression crossed his face that said very plainly he had noticed something of importance. He flickered a glance at me, a sort of warning glance, so it was something he did not wish to share with Morley. The man soon left, deciding not to go up to London after all. I doubt there was any luggage stored in his carriage. He had gone as far as he intended going that day, unless he meant to try his luck with Gwynne if Kessler failed him. Such eagerness to secure the help of outsiders confirmed his innocence.

"What is it you noticed on that envelope?" I asked Ludwig as soon as it was possible.

"That note wasn't in Mrs. Knightsbridge's handwriting," he said. "I saw her letter of recommendation for Miss Smith, and the writing was markedly different. A very pretty, flowing script she used. Florid."

"What!"

"All loops and swirls—almost an artform itself."

"Oh," I said, in a weak voice.

"What's the matter?"

"Nothing." How was it possible he hadn't seen my

cards of invitation, hadn't heard Abbie and Annie mention their artistic loops and swirls? *I* was Mrs. Knightsbridge! A married woman, as I had known all along. I must tell him. How could I do it? Such a deceitful creature, this Mrs. Knightsbridge, whom I really detested, if the truth were known. The very name set my hackles up. No wonder I hated me. Keeping this knowledge from Sir Ludwig, and he had done so much for me. It was infamous. *I* was infamous, a deceitful, lying kidnapper.

I made sure he would soon tumble to it that as Miss Smith was not Mrs. Knightsbridge, *I* was. But no, he wouldn't let it occur to himself. He came up with another explanation, quite ingenious I must admit.

"Mrs. Knightsbridge might have monkeyed around with that character reference, but she didn't write the ransom note. I believe Uxbridge did it himself and signed her name to it. It is the only explanation."

I should tell him. I *should!* I hinted at it, without quite putting it in black and white. "Maybe Miss Empey wrote it—Miss Empey is Miss Smith, I mean."

"Oh no, you recall Miss Smith wore the fur-lined cape, indicating she was a grand lady."

"*I* wore the silken petticoats," I mentioned.

"Yes, so you did. You are thinking *you* are Mrs. Knightsbridge?"

I nodded. It had been agreed I was one or the other. It had also been agreed the villain in the piece was the employer—me.

"Well, even if you are, which I don't believe for a minute, we don't know any worse of the woman but that she wrote a letter changing her companion's name. We don't know *why* she did it, don't know any actual harm of her."

"That's true," I said, wanting to believe him. There was some detail nagging at the back of my mind, but with such a multitude of great thundering troubles, it didn't quite surface. "The letter from Mrs. Knightsbridge —the character letter—how did you say it was signed?"

"Mrs. J.F. Knightsbridge, I believe. Why do you ask?"

"I wondered if she had signed her Christian name."

"No, her husband's initials, in the usual way."

But if the husband's initials were J.F., who was Ivor, who took an interest in my petticoats? Was I a philanderess, along with the rest?

Chapter Thirteen

I went to my room, claiming a headache, not entirely falsely, pitched myself onto my bed and worried in a manner that would have put Mr. Morley to shame. I was a wretch. Here was I, foisting myself onto poor unwitting Sir Ludwig when I knew perfectly well I was Mrs. Knightsbridge. Letting him fall in love with me and worry over me and believe me a poor put-upon companion, when I was a wealthy woman who was involved in this messy business for more gain. I didn't think it was money I was after. I wanted Miss Grafton's share of the Medici triptych, and my ultimate goal was to get my hands on it. Why I had asked for money in lieu of it I had no idea (or had Miss Empey do so, surely on my behalf), but I knew that my real motive in this business was to get the painting. Since seeing Gwynne's madonna, I had coveted it. I had dreamed of my portion of it one night—all in good clear detail, as it was well known to me, Mrs. Knightsbridge, who owned the main panel. Whatever I had been doing roaming the roads late at night, it had to do with getting Gwynne's piece of the thing. I was the brains behind it; I felt it in my bones.

I was so mortified with myself, hated Mrs. Knightsbridge so very thoroughly, was so ashamed to have to face Sir Ludwig with the truth that I decided to disappear in the same mysterious manner in which I had come to Wickey. I would leave. Period. I didn't know where I would go. Certainly turning myself over to the authorities was the farthest thing from my mind. Evading them was more like it. Edinburgh was there, not as a first stop, but one that must be taken in. It would require careful scouting to discover if there was a warrant out for my arrest before I went dashing to the north. Once Williker returned with a description of me, there was no hope of concealing the truth. Meanwhile, I would require some money to make good my escape, and wondered how I was to excuse yet another loan from Sir Ludwig, my only possible source.

I knew that somewhere, hidden so well she had not come to light in over a month, my poor Miss Empey was holding Miss Grafton captive, waiting to receive orders from me. What must she have been thinking all these weeks? No wonder the note had taken so long to come. My amnestic state had badly interfered with my plans. And *that*, very likely, accounted for the feelings of anger that swelled up in me upon occasions. I couldn't help Miss Empey or the Grafton girl—hadn't a single clue where they might be, but I could help myself and Sir Ludwig by a timely disappearance, and hope that eventually Miss Empey would turn Lorraine Grafton free.

I don't know how Sir Ludwig spent his day. He went into the village at one point, and came back with the story that the mysterious man of undistinguished appearance had been seen again. He claimed this was the reason I must leave, but I think he had actually done some sober thinking and knew, or suspected, that I was Mrs. Knightsbridge. Knew I was a criminal and wanted to hide me somewhere I couldn't be arrested when Mr. Williker showed up, as he must very soon now. In any case, he put forward a plan that suited my ends very well. I was to be taken to a small farm he owned on the south coast of England, only forty miles away, but that was far enough away that, if done with secrecy, I would not be found. He mentioned the man's attack in the garden, but I doubted he had even heard the man was back in Wickey. Who *could* that man have been? Another teasing little riddle within the puzzle of Mrs. Knightsbridge.

"We'll leave tonight, after dark," Ludwig said. "In that way you'll be safe till Williker gets here and we can get this thing sorted out. Try not to worry, Rose. I would stay with you if I could, but I must be in touch with Morley about the ransom. I plan to go to see him tomorrow. The housekeeper and her husband will be with you. It is a holiday house for us in the summer, right on the coast. Not the best time of the year for it, in January, but you'll be safe there."

In my eagerness to be away, I snatched at the offer. It would be easier to slip away from a housekeeper and her husband than himself. I'd get away, somehow, and never have to face him again. "Do I go alone?" I asked.

"I'm taking you. Would you like Abbie to go for company?"

"No—it might be best if things go on as much like normal as possible here," I answered quickly, wanting no impediments to my flight.

"That's what I thought. I planned to have Abbie go into Wickey tomorrow and mention you are ill with a cold, to give the impression you are still here, in case that fellow's still after you. She suggested stopping at the pharmacy and getting some medicines for you. I didn't suggest Annie as a companion. She rattles on so."

"I'll take my paints and do a seascape to pass the time."

"Do it from the window. Don't go out, just in case. It

will be cold and damp and very breezy there on the coast, in any case. It will be only for a day or two, till I see Williker, and arrange about the ransom for Morley. I mean, by hook or by crook, to follow whoever picks up the money and find out where Miss Grafton is put away."

I packed up my belongings, eked out to require a small valise by this time, and went belowstairs to say goodbye to Annie and Abbie. They were excited, but not distressed, not aware then of my true identity. There wasn't an opportunity to borrow money—how should I account for needing it, stuck in a cottage from which I was told not to budge? I must make do with the few bits of change I had left over from other shopping trips. I just noticed, sitting on the edge of a hall table, a note left by me to the cook regarding some supplies ordered for that elaborate fiasco of a New Year's party. The flowing script caught my eye. That it should be out here, where it had not been before, told me the matter had been under discussion between Ludwig and the ladies. They knew who I really was, then, but did not guess the whole, of course.

I wondered just how much Ludwig had figured out. This trip told me he at least suspected I was in trouble with the law. If only I had been informed of all his doings that day, of Morley's return, for instance, I might not have engaged in my precipitous flight from Bay House, as his seaside home was called. I wonder how things would have turned out if I hadn't. My memory must have come back sooner or later; I would have learned the truth, and some unpleasantness might have been avoided. I personally deserved any unpleasantness God or Fate chose to heap on me, but there was no earthly reason Sir Ludwig should have received such a quantity of it.

The trip was almost pleasant, except that I kept thinking I would never see him again. We left at ten, traveling the better part of the night, averaging under seven miles an hour over the icy roads despite a team of four. It was cold, but bright, with the moon picking out eerie scenes, black trees etched against the silver sky. Within, we had our fur rugs and hot bricks for our feet, and best of all, for these few hours, we had each other. It was no great magnanimous decision on my part to admit my knowledge of who I was. He already knew, or strongly suspected from that piece of my handwriting. Still, to clear the air between us, I told him my theory.

"I know that is what you have been thinking. You may be right," he allowed. And all that time he *knew*, and didn't tell me. "I went to see Gwynne today. I don't believe I mentioned it to you. He knows Mrs. Knightsbridge—by reputation I mean—and he has the notion she is a widow. That is possible you know, Rose."

It was almost heartbreaking to see him so determined to make me eligible, clutching at any straw. Heartwrenching too for me to wish so hard he were right. "Where did he get that idea?"

"He doesn't know exactly. It is mostly that all references to the museum in Scotland mention Mrs. Knightsbridge. The husband never crops up at all. One would think that if there were a Mr. Knightsbridge still alive he would feature more prominently in its doings. Williker too, you recall, mentioned a secretary—this Soames fellow—but never a word about Mr. Knightsbridge. I really think he is no longer living."

"It would be easy enough to find out," I said, half allowing myself to hope. But wife or widow, I was still a criminal.

"Williker will know. If you had a husband, surely he would have been making enquiries for you. He wouldn't let you be gone over a month without any word, without looking for you. He must have known where you were headed, and there have been no notices in any papers saying you are missing."

"And that would explain Ivor!" I said, trying eagerly to blot out any of my sins I could.

"How would it explain him?"

"Well, Ivor is not J.F. Knightsbridge, and I thought it was pretty horrid of me to be saying Ivor would be concerned about my petticoats when I had a husband, but if I am a widow . . ."

"He's a lover, you mean?" The voice in the darkness was harsh.

"Don't say it like that, Ludwig! It's not as bad as a married woman having one. I hadn't met you then, you know."

Across the space between the banquettes his hands reached out for mine and held them. "Let it be firmly understood, Mrs. Knightsbridge, I have first bid, if it turns out you *are* a widow."

"We had better wait and see what else I am first," I suggested, growing despondent again to consider it all.

"No, love, I am convinced you would not keep so close a tab on what you owe me if you were a hardened crook," he answered, trying to cheer me.

"It's *you* who is always keeping track of my bill."

"Keeping you at Granhurst by indenture, you see."

We talked for the first hour, then as the swaying of the carriage and the late hour combined with darkness to induce drowsiness, I curled up in a corner to sleep, and Ludwig did the same. I awoke, perhaps an hour later, to find he had removed to my banquette and had an arm around me. It was very comfortable, having his chest for a pillow.

"Rose, are you awake?" he asked softly. I must have stirred and awoke him.

"Half," I mumbled.

"Try to sleep," he suggested, tightening his arms around me. I let on I was. I knew, married woman that I was, that he really wanted to make love to me. The gentle, stroking of his hands on my back and arms was far from sleep-inducing. A single move would have him telling us I was a widow, and I would be obliged to make him sit on the other bench, when I wanted at least the comfort of his arms around me. Some time

162

later I did doze off again, and didn't awaken till the horses pulled up in front of a cottage set back a hundred yards from the sea.

It was roughly four o'clock in the morning when we arrived, yet the place was lit up. "Oh, they are expecting us," I exclaimed, surprised. I had the impression our coming here was taken on the spur of the moment.

"I sent word on ahead," he answered, helping me down from the carriage, while a cold blast of air from the sea warned me how the weather would be in this area.

I hardly bothered to glance at the house's exterior—it was of stone, with a large verandah running around the front which would be pleasant for sitting out in the summer. Snow had blown into the corners of it, and been glazed down to ice from the moisture-laden sea air and the bitter winds. Pitted ice, due of course to the salt in the sea air. The front door was wet with frost forming around the handle and lock, giving an odd feeling of entering a house made of ice. Within, it was cosy, with a cheery fire blazing in a huge open hearth in the main room. The decor was rustic, wood paneling without much in the way of carving, brightly colored sofas and chairs. It was a warm, inelegant family holiday house, that suited the Kesslers better than their regular home. What good times they must have here in summer, I thought, with a pang of regret that I would never be joining them.

The housekeeper and her spouse, the Peterses, were both in attendance. The latter went to the stable to see the grooms had what they required, while the former made us comfortable and went to bring food and something hot to drink. Mrs. Peters was a middle-aged, cheerful woman, a little inclined to stoutness, rather highly colored in complexion. She was a good cook, as her figure suggested. We enjoyed a filling and delicious *pot au feu,* which she humbly called 'leftovers,' with fresh-made bread. Mrs. Feilotter could learn a few tricks from her. It was odd how I still went on, in my mind, managing the household affairs of this family. As dawn began to break, I was told it was time for bed. Sir Ludwig was not to remain. He wanted to be back at Granhurst by a decent hour, for he had a full day ahead of him. I realized then, too late, what an imposition it had been for me to take for granted he would deliver me here. With Mrs. Peters looking on I could hardly tell him so. We left with no more than a mention that we would be meeting again soon. Ironic words! This was good bye, not *au revoir*.

I went to bed planning to cry, but was so tired I fell sound asleep within minutes. It was not till morning that the full sum of my loss hit me. It was just as well I had plans of my own to sustain me, for I wanted to do nothing more than turn my head into the fat pillow and bawl.

It is surprising how helpless one feels without money. I had not found an opportunity to borrow any, so I got out my change purse and counted up all my odd shillings and pence. It came to a little over two pounds—all accounted for in Sir Ludwig's books, of course. To contemplate a long trip with such meager resources was a daunting experience. My first thought was still to leave—to get away and sort out my life. I wondered if I dared resort to Soames or my mysterious Ivor by letter for funds. But not from here. First I had to leave Bay House. With this end in view, I asked the Peterses for a map. There were extensive chartings of the local area available, including marine maps, but of the island as a whole, the island of England, I had to make do with a map in a geography book found in the schoolroom. London seemed a good spot to lose myself in. Williker had mentioned in his letter I had been heading there. I couldn't imagine why, but once there, something might occur to me. I must have friends or business associates. Some doorway might beckon.

A careful but casual conversation with Mrs. Peters told me what I had to know. We were off the main road by two miles. In order to catch a stage to anywhere, one had to get to the main road. London was of no interest to her. I don't think she had ever been there, but she occasionally got as far as Southampton, and told me readily enough how to reach it, from which larger center transportation to London would be available. I had not arisen till ten-thirty. By the time I had steered the conversation past the shoals of her being lonesome and cut off and getting ready to visit a friend, another hour had passed, and the coach would be passing any minute. The next would be at three in the afternoon. I must catch this one. I had no desire to wait for the night stage, to be standing alone in the middle of the road, frightened and freezing at two in the morning. My two pounds would more than get me to Southampton, and from there on I must improvise.

To pass the next hours, I decided to go out and have a look at the beach, despite Sir Ludwig's warnings. The weather had turned much milder. The glazing outside had melted in the sun, and the ocean breezes were not at all soul-destroying. Nothing would do but Mr. Peters must accompany me on my stroll. He was but a poor companion, having not a word or a single piece of information to relay unless one asked a direct question. He was an excellent watchdog, however. I could not so much as go for a look behind a rock without having him at my heels. Sir Ludwig, I assumed, had spoken to him about guarding me. This made my escape difficult indeed. Time to leave to catch the three o'clock stage came and went, with either Mr. or Mrs. Peters constantly hovering over me. In desperation, I went to my room at three, claiming fatigue, with the hope that I might get out by a window and flee. What must Mr. Peters do but station himself in the front yard, hammering on some box, but taking frequent peeks in the direction of my window. Had I been too indiscreet with my questions about maps and transportation? I had made it all sound logical, wanting to see exactly where I was, and so on. It almost began to seem they knew what I was up to. Even, the idea came to me, that I was a prisoner.

But if I were a prisoner, my window had no bars, and I was determined by some means I would get out it and meet the two a.m. stage to Southampton. I went to my room early after dinner, for the watching eyes of my two guardians were wearing my nerves thin. I lay on my bed, and thought in a disjointed and far-ranging manner of my predicament. At eleven, the Peterses retired. By twelve, there wasn't a sound in the dark house. At the window, the moon shone mistily through a veil of clouds. I thanked God it was not pitch black, was not too cold, was not snowing, as it had been that other night I had to walk alone along dark roads, to a destination equally uncertain to my present one. At one, by the clock on the dresser, I put on my cloak and began working on the window. It was difficult to raise, but after a few tugs that hurt my shoulder joints it slid up and I felt the cool touch of the night air on my face. Peering into the front yard, I saw it to be free of Mr. Peters. I would not have been much surprised to see him there, still hammering on that box.

I clambered out the window, hung by my finger tips with my legs dangling down the wall of the house till they nearly touched the verandah roof, which slanted down to within jumping distance of the ground. I feared I had lost my footing on the roof and was about to tumble head over heels, causing a great racket, as well as giving me a sprained something or other. But my footing was regained fairly quietly. I shimmied my way to the edge of the roof, crouched to jump. It seemed suddenly a higher leap than I had planned on. I sat on the edge, steeled myself for it, and plunged. Nothing hurt. I was off and running, down the drive, out onto the road. No sooner had I taken four paces in the direction of the stage stop than I heard feet pounding after me.

Mr. Peters, standing on guard to stop me? *Was* I a prisoner then? In any case, I was a fleeing prisoner, and I ran as I had never run in my life before. There was nothing that could properly be called a thought in my head, just a great black ball of fear, panic, and determination to outrun whoever was coming after me, faster, faster, till I could hear him gasp for breath. The absurd, nightmarish notion cropped into my head that it was my past pursuing me. Or was it my foe from the chapel grounds? The road surface was perfectly treacherous. Wet with slush crusted to ice in little peaks formed by wheels of carriages passing earlier, every inch holding a trap in the blind darkness. At least the disadvantage worked both ways. I heard my pursuer slip, curse, and regain his footing, and again he was coming after me, gaining inch by inch as my legs fought against clumsy long skirts. Another dark form darted out of the bushes by the roadside in front of me. It was Mr. Peters.

"Get her! Stop her!" the man behind me shouted in an angry voice. "Don't let the bitch get away." The sound of that voice brought me to a dead halt. It was impossible, but it was Sir Ludwig Kessler.

Chapter Fourteen

Once I came to a stop, it was no time till I was apprehended, of course. I stood there in the cold roadway, trying to see the face of this man I had trusted, had thought a friend, more than a friend. Vision was imperfect, but clear enough to show me a glowering white mask. "Congratulations, Mrs. Knightsbridge, on an excellent performance," he said, then grabbed my arm rudely, while Mr. Peters wordlessly took my other, and in this manner I was dragged back to Bay House. They moved so quickly speech was impossible. I couldn't think of a word to say, in any case.

"Lock her in her room," Ludwig said in that hard voice I hardly recognized. "I'll bring the police in the morning." As an afterthought he added, "And Peters, nail some boards over the window. Do it now, at once."

"Why am I being locked up?" I demanded.

"Better get used to it, Mrs. Knightsbridge," Sir Ludwig replied in a sneering voice. "With luck, you'll only get ten years in Bridewell and escape the gibbet." Then he stalked from the room. I'm sure I don't know where he could be going, in the middle of the night, but he went outside.

Peters, perhaps not relishing the job of climbing on a roof and indulging in carpentry in the middle of the night, locked me in the attic instead. He threw a blanket at me before closing the door, as though I were a dog. I half expected it to be followed by a bone. It is difficult to say what my sensations were during the next hours. They were too confused. I had been brought here not for safety then, but to be locked up, a prisoner as I half thought all along. Sir Ludwig *knew* I was Mrs. Knightsbridge, must have known all along, and apparently knew a great deal more as well. Knew I was ripe for prison, so must know I was behind Miss Grafton's kidnapping. But why had I been treated so royally at Granhurst? Had he been working with Morley and the police all the while? Yes, I had been kept under pretty close surveillance there as well, when I considered it. If he knew me for a criminal, why had he let me stay on, with his cousin and vulnerable sister? The house had seemed familiar to me from the very beginning. I began to wonder if I had been going there when I got off the coach. This line was futile, however. I could make nothing of it. Nor could I make any sense of the way in which I had been treated—like a member of the family, and not the least-loved, either.

I was not so foolish as to try to sleep. I wrapped the blanket over my shoulders. Between it and my warm cloak I was not quite freezing, though my fingers and toes would have welcomed a fire, and my eyes would have appreciated some light. It was very dark in the attic in the dead of night, with only a faint glow from the clouded moon penetrating dusty, small windows. The windows were investigated for possibility of escape, but in vain. High up, with no access to the ground except by flight. At length I stopped pacing and sat on a hard trunk, bundled into my blanket. At least I knew who I was. I was Mrs. J.F. Knightsbridge, from

Edinburgh. A wealthy lady who dabbled in the arts for a pastime. I wondered how hard the law would be on such a lady. Someone said the law was a cobweb that caught midges and let through hornets. I hoped Mrs. J.F. Knightsbridge was wealthy enough to be considered a hornet. Wondered too exactly what crime I would be standing trial for, now that I was caught. Not just the kidnapping—there was extortion as well to go along with it. Surely to God I had not ordered Lorraine Grafton murdered! No—*no*, this I could not believe of myself.

I didn't sleep a wink the rest of the night. I saw the sun rise over the naked trees, a golden rose dawn it was, with purple shadows. I thought it would make a lovely painting, except that the true drama of nature was too contrived to look well in a picture. No one would believe it. No one would even tackle it, except possibly Fuseli. At seven, Mr. Peters came and led me downstairs to my room, which had been decorated with the wooden bars over my window. I shuddered inwardly. 'Better get used to it, Mrs. Knightsbridge.' I soon got used to it. By the time breakfast came, I was quite accustomed to peering between the slats, down the road, for signs of—what? Police I suppose, coming to take me to a different prison. I was not at all repentant, but only angry that I had been caught, and that I could not even remember what it was I had done.

It was infamous, unjust, and not to be borne. I considered my plight in what I thought was a logical manner, and came to the conclusion it could not well be worse than it was. I was to stand trial with no means of defending myself. Whatever motives had caused me to break the law, I could not put them forward. I observed that Mr. Peters lurked around the front of the house, not always in my sight, but often enough so that I knew he skulked there, to be sure I didn't pry off my bars and leap again. As no sign or sound of Kessler had been observed since my return, I assumed that when he left the front door the night before he had left the area. It was only the Peterses guarding me. I was not likely to be so little guarded again. When luncheon came—at least they weren't starving me—it would be brought by my jailers. I would hope for Mrs. Peters, tap her on the head, lock her in with her own key, and leave.

I sat patiently waiting for lunch. At noon on the dot I heard her ascend the stairs on her soft feet, set down the tray outside the door, move the key in the lock and peek her head in. She looked frightfully embarrassed, the one look I got at her before lowering a flower pot on her head, from my hiding place behind the door. A geranium it was, that had been turning yellow on the window ledge. She fell forward, not unconscious, but dazed enough for me to dart out and turn the key that was still in the lock. I was all ready, cloak on, plans made. Off down the stairs, out the back door to evade Mr. Peters watching my window from the front. It was miraculously simple, except that once out I had nowhere to go.

The afternoon coach was not due till three, and long before that they would be out looking for me. As soon as Mrs. Peters got the window raised and hollered to her husband. They would know where to look, too, thanks to my questions. I took off like the wind, running in a southerly direction, though I didn't know it. Bay House was halfway down the western slit of that little inlet of the ocean that sticks like a knife into the belly of the south coast, with the Isle of Wight guarding the open end. I kept peering over my shoulder, wondering that I was not followed. I later learned that Mrs. Peters, a confirmed ninnyhammer, didn't have the sense to raise the window and shout. She spent fifteen minutes picking the door lock open with a hairpin, only because her husband was not at that moment visible from the window. I believe he took his job of jailer rather negligently, sitting on the verandah half the time to escape the wind.

After running for about half a mile, gaining sharp stabbing pains in my chest and gasping for breath, I saw a small village rising before me in the distance. Not more than a dozen buildings, it offered poor concealment, but there was a largish boat just preparing to put off from the shore. I asked at once where it was heading, hoping for France and safety. The sailor told me to Hythe, a mile down the coast, thence to the Isle of Wight, to deliver nails and paint for the shipbuilding industry. Excellent! Who would be looking for me on the Isle of Wight? The police, as soon as they discovered my trick, but an island of over a hundred square miles with several thousands of population seemed at that hectic moment a safer refuge than the public roads. I begged to be allowed to go, claiming urgent business on Wight. I didn't quibble over the fee, though it was of course somewhat higher than the customary one. The man was ready to leave on the instant, and I didn't intend for the ship to get away without me. I regretted the stop at Hythe, but it was extremely brief indeed, only to drop off a few packages and pick up a passenger. A nondescript person, a businessman.

The gentleman introduced himself as soon as the ropes were cast off, and it was soon evident he meant to make a pest of himself. He was that obtrusive sort who insists on telling a stranger all his business, and clearly expects to hear one's own in return. I soon learned Mr. Colroy had three drapery shops on the island, and was on his way back from a buying spree in London, where the woolens, he told me, had reached a shocking price. He blushed to ask the sum from his customers. Then his light blue eyes examined me with interest, waiting to hear my story. I became Miss Jones (rather tired of being Miss Smith), on my way to visit an aunt, also Miss Jones, at Cowes, as that was the port to which we were headed.

"I have a shop there," Mr. Colroy told me at once. "The Colroy Drapery Shop, on the main street. I believe I know your aunt."

"Oh!" I said in dismay, till I realized that outside of a

Miss Smith, there was no inhabitant for any village more likely than a Miss Jones.

I was soon claiming kin to a host of Joneses, stretched from Cowes to Ventnor on the island's south coast. Mr. Colroy and I were old friends by the time the ship docked. As I had no real friend in the place, I began wondering if I might not put Mr. Colroy to use. I began dropping hints that my aunt did not actually expect me, and I was the most shatterbrained thing in nature not to have waited a reply to my letter before coming. I meant to surprise her for her birthday, I told him, smiling stupidly.

"You can always take the next boat back to the mainland if she's not there," he consoled me.

"Yes," I was forced to agree aloud, but my mind was busy circumventing this sane and logical course. What I had decided to do was to find myself employment with Mr. Colroy at one or the other of his three shops, or his own house. Just what the eventual outcome of this was to be was unclear, but it would give me time and a little money. I could, in the breathing space, write to Mr. Soames from there and if I were not being sought by police, he would send money or even come and get me.

Just before we parted at the dock, I wangled a half-hearted invitation from Mr. Colroy. "Well, if your aunt isn't home, you can be in touch with me at the inn, the Wight Arms, where I mean to eat before going on to Newport. That is where I live, outside of Newport. I can lend you a little something if you are short," he offered. I had intimated a shortage of cash to get back to the mainland. He looked so respectable that it was impossible to suspect any ulterior motive in his offer. Indeed I had to all but burst into tears before he extended it.

I walked along the main street till I got to the Colroy Drapery Shop. It *did* exist, which lent my Mr. Colroy a very respectable coloring, for it was quite a fine shop. I let another quarter hour slip by, time to visit Auntie

Jones and learn she was gone to the mainland to visit relatives, before going to the Wight Arms and asking for Mr. Colroy. He was in the dining room, lucky man. I was led to him and at once outlined my predicament. "Oh dear," he said, shaking his head at such unwonted goings-on. "Well, I shall be happy to lend you a little something. I must get on to Newport at once myself, or I would see you safely onto the boat." He was already reaching for his wallet.

Newport, right in the middle of the island I had learned, a good central location from which to run his three shops, sounded infinitely more safe and concealing than Cowes. I was always a bit of a fast talker, and with the urgency of getting away with him, leaving at once, I had soon invented an aunt, another Miss Jones, in Newport. She too must be away when I arrived, but by then I hoped to have him well around my finger, and get a temporary post with him while awaiting my aunt's return. He appeared to be the most gullible of God's creations. He swallowed this string of lies without a flicker of his blue eyes, and offered me a seat in his carriage. I rather hoped he would offer a bite of lunch as well, but he didn't. He went on eating stolidly before my hungry eyes, chicken in a brown sauce, mashed potatoes, green peas. Lovely breads. He did not take dessert, but had a cup of coffee.

I believe towards the end of the meal it occurred to him I had not eaten. I didn't try to conceal it, but gazed soulfully on his delicious looking chicken. He was in a great hurry, however, and by the time he asked, rather apologetically, whether I had lunched, and I quickly assured him I had not, he had nearly finished his coffee.

"I am most eager to get home," he explained. "Would you care to have a sandwich wrapped to eat in the carriage?"

Indeed I would, along with a piece of the plum cake I saw going to other tables. A carafe of coffee was added as well, in a glass bottle of the sort used for preserving fruit. I was afraid Colroy would make some comment about my lack of luggage, but he seemed rather distracted, his mind probably on business. I ate hungrily once the carriage was rolling, for it was well into the afternoon by this time and I had had nothing since breakfast. Mr. Colroy's chaise was not so elegant as Kessler's. We had a somewhat mangy fur rug, but no hot bricks. The coffee was still warm, however, and quite delicious, a little sweeter than I liked. It made me think of Annie. I must not fall into the foolish habit of wishing I were back at Granhurst with my friendly jailers. Still, with the food and warm drink in my stomach, I found myself going back there, in my mind. I yawned luxuriously, and felt sleepy enough to have a nap. Hadn't closed an eye all night, I remembered lazily. My troubles suddenly seemed faraway, trivial. Mr. Colroy aroused from his reverie and commented, "You look drowsy," in a fatherly way. "Why don't you finish up your coffee? It will waken you up."

I didn't particularly want to wake up, but I finished the coffee, as it was already poured into my cup.

That is the last thing I remember before coming to some hours later with a splitting headache, tied up on a bed in a perfectly black room, with a gag in my mouth, feeling utterly confused and frightened.

Chapter Fifteen

Someone is trying to kill me. That much I think is clear now. The attack outside the chapel and the drugged coffee—no accidents or misadventures, but attempts by the same hand to do away with me. Why? Surely of all the harmless people in this great big world, no one could be more harmless than a girl who doesn't even know her own name.

What nonsense! Of *course* I know my own name. 'Elizabeth Grant is in a rant!' The children used to chant those words at me when I went to school. They made fun of me for something, mean little beasts. They were jealous because I lived in the best house in the village. Used to—

'Elizabeth Grant is in a rant
Her mammy's dead and she lives with her aunt.'
I felt a scalding tear start in my eye—Mammy was dead all over again, and I was thrown into that *wretched* dame school for the children to point and poke at me. Laugh at my fancy gowns, that became progressively less fancy as I outgrew them, and they were replaced

by Aunt Jessica. God, how I hated those fustian gowns. 'You don't want to stand out from the others!' Jessica informed me. But I *did*. I didn't want to be Elizabeth Grant, in a rant, with Mammy dead. I wanted to go back home, up on the hill. I shivered—I didn't want to remember any more.

How cold it was here. This must be an attic. As my eyes adjusted to the gloom, I distinguished one rectangle an infinitesimal fraction lighter than the rest of the blackness. A window, the glass divided into twelve small panes. Very like the windows in my own office. A fear gripped me. In all the chill, perspiration popped out on my forehead, my upper lip, deformed with this foul-smelling rag. I must be rid of it before anything else. Frenzied jaw motions and tongue pushings succeeded in loosening the gag. A shoulder proved useful in dislodging it till at last I could breathe properly. Great lung-filling gulps of the cold air were swallowed greedily.

I glanced again to the window, half expecting to see it had disappeared. It had become clearer. One pane of glass was broken. No wonder I froze here, with no covering but my cloak. My fur-lined cape should be warmer. My chin, brushing the coverlet, told me it was not my own—it had a rough texture. Ah, but of course, it would be the one I wore to fool Mr. Gwynne. Why was it I wanted to fool him? It was Kitty's idea. It had something to do with the missing madonna. Oh, but my head ached! Everything, every memory dissolved with the pain of it.

I closed my eyes to rest and sleep. When I awakened, the rectangle of window was markedly lighter. It was navy blue, the rest of the room still black. My head cleared, and suddenly I knew exactly who I was. Elizabeth Knightsbridge, and still in a rant. Jumbled pictures from a past life darted into my head, each clear and sharp-edged like a *trompe l'oeil* painting, but with no coherence, in jumbled order. Elizabeth Grant, yelling and screaming at ten was followed immediately by some pale-cheeked woman standing at an altar in a chapel in Italy, with delightful frescoes all around her, being married to John, and grieving, grieving in her heart—is it for the marriage or for the death? I thought my mind deceived me still. Why was I marrying a man with silver hair? Kitty's voice, authoritative, firm, pealed in my ear. "It was your father's intention, and wish, Beth. Indeed I see no way out of it. John has already given him a great deal of money as your settlement, to cover his more pressing obligations. And how are you to go on, alone in a foreign country?" I see Papa being bowled over by a passing coach, see his head hit the cobblestones, see the red blood . . . No, I won't think of that. All right, Father died of an accident in Florence and I was left alone, without funds.

How had I got to Florence? I had some dim, shadowy pictures, why were they growing dimmer? of a wretched scene at school, and later at home with Aunt Jessica. Yes, it was the McCurdle sisters—no! Not elderly spinsters at a dame school. Two sisters then not yet grown into gossiping spinsters, practicing up their craft on me, while I rose to every taunt. Blushed for my fustian gown, railed at being rooted out of my own fine home, and insisted my father *did* love me, and would take me out of this horrid place very soon and buy me a silken gown. Oh yes, my gowns and appearances meant a great deal to me. They meant security, and Mama and safety. They meant escaping that school and Aunt Jessica. Well, Papa *did* love me. When he sobered up from the monumental drunk following Mama's death, he had taken me away, away forever from Aunt Jessica and that school.

I suspected the reason I couldn't understand why we had lost our home when Mama died was that I never had been told. It had always been Mama's family that bailed us out, and maybe they were not of a mind to go on bailing once Mama was gone. So we drifted, Papa and I, floated across seas and international boundaries like a pair of vagabonds, buying and selling paintings, painting a portrait ourselves upon occasion, but always with 'the dice against us,' as Papa said. The 'Rembrandt' bought for a song would be worth exactly what we paid for it, while the dark old religious painting that reminded one vaguely of Caravaggio but of course couldn't possibly *be* his work, Papa would sell cheap, only to read in the papers next week that the Comte de Planat had come upon an unknown Caravaggio worth thousands.

So I married Mr. John Knightsbridge, because he was quite determined to have me, and because my father had borrowed money from him, a fellow Briton met by accident at an art auction in Florence. We always loved Florence, Papa and I, till we met the Knightsbridges, that is. Papa told me John wanted to marry me, told me one day we were driving about the countryside, and had stopped at an olive orchard—hot and dry and dusty—to try to sell the owner a set of candlesticks that we called Berninis. I married a man not much younger than my father, and as well as married his aunt, too. Kitty Empey, his mother's youngest sister, formed an integral part of our household from the beginning. John and I might have dealt much better without her. I shouldn't feel all this angry aversion, for John had been kind to me, treated me more generously than I had ever been treated since Mama's death.

We traveled for a year, Kitty and John and myself, selecting purchases for the Knightsbridge Museum, to be opened as soon as we returned to Edinburgh. The timely conclusion of the war had even allowed us to finish our tour in Paris, which had been inundated with Englishmen like ourselves to celebrate the victory. I didn't want to leave it and go back to Edinburgh. Who lived in *Scotland*? It was cold and damp, with nothing but rocks and heather and sheep. I used often to dream of rocks and sheep in the days following my marriage, yet I had seen little enough of them after I was married. We lived a civilized, urbane existence, in a fine mansion in the fashionable district of Edinburgh.

The days were busy and happy, the evenings held many social engagements, and if it had not been for the late nights, alone with John, I could have been happy. A girl of eighteen married to a gentleman of forty-two whom she does not love cannot ever be *quite* happy, however. She will feel cheated of romance, and while she will remain faithful to her silver-haired husband if she is not an outright villain (which I hope I am not), she will not be able to control her eyes just as she ought. A smile warmer than it should be will occasionally escape her lips, to cause jealousy and scenes, and even to set up the hackles of one's husband's family and friends.

I am afraid I set up a good number of hackles. John's uncle Jeremy called me quite bluntly 'that wench picked up in a foreign country,' while an aunt married to a bishop tried her hand at arranging an annulment. All their anger and schemes came to naught. John fooled them and died in his forty-fourth year of pneumonia. Kitty blamed it on a broken heart, and I blamed it on her talking him into remaining in cold Scotland when both John and I had wanted to go back to Italy. I believe the relatives would have cut me off on the spot had I not been in an 'interesting condition.' I was with child, but miscarried in my third month. What a horrid thing to say, but I was not completely sorry.

Kitty Empey had no thought of cutting herself off from me, nor had I the means of severing myself from her, either. John's will proved a cunning document that left all to me, the mansion, the money (and there was plenty of it), the museum, providing I gave a home to Kitty for as long as she lived, and providing I not remarry. Upon any remarriage, I lost everything but one hundred pounds. I think only the very *meanest* of minds would have bothered with that addendum. What is a hundred pounds? It would prevent the world from saying he cut me off without a penny, and John cared a good deal what the world said. He was always harping on it, but of course over the months I had come to manage him pretty well. With such a carefully controlled fortune, suitors proved as scarce as whales' feathers. Bereft of child and independence, I threw myself into running the museum, opened two years ago and dedicated to my husband, John Francis Knightsbridge. Kitty did the same, and proved useful as she knew a great deal about art. She had far-flung associates in the art world, including a Mr. Grafton, of Gillingham, with whom her family was connected somehow on Mrs. Grafton's side. They frequently corresponded, comparing opinions on acquisitions, the suitability of prices offered on various works up for sale, the choice of an expert to authenticate a painting, and so on.

It was through Kitty's correspondence with Mr. Grafton that we learned he possessed one door of our Medici triptych, purchased by my father in Italy and left to me, his sole worldly possession of any monetary worth. We were eager to acquire the Grafton door, but it was not only the door that precipitated our visit south. A number of matters conjoined to bring it about. I, always eager to escape Edinburgh and the family, wished to visit London. Friends of John's and mine were stopping with us on a visit to the Highlands, and extended an offer to me to return to London with them. The Mayhews it was, a youngish couple met in Germany during our honeymoon. I hoped to get away from Kitty for a few months, but there was never any escaping her. She received a letter from Miss Grafton that decided her to join us on the trip south, though not necessarily to London.

Miss Grafton feared her guardian, Mr. Morley, was mismanaging her estate, not purposely but through ignorance. At sixteen, she did not know a great deal about art yet herself, but she knew her uncle had sold two paintings her father treasured, and had got a low price for them. She knew as well that Miss Empey was considered quite an authority by her father, and asked her advice as to what she should do. It was enough. With no real life of her own, Kitty was always eager to interfere in another's. She would go herself and look into the matter. She took the notion, always thinking the worst of everyone, that Morley was not ignorant but a scoundrel who was pocketing Miss Grafton's money. While there, she was to try for the door of the Medici triptych for the museum. We left her off at Gillingham, where we all stopped overnight. She went incognito on the public tour of the Grafton collection that Monday and managed to make herself known to Miss Lorraine Grafton. Her keen eyes had picked out the Giorgione forgery, and she learned from the girl that her father had believed it to be genuine. Grafton was certainly thought to have purchased the original, and Kitty could not feel he had been gammoned by this copy. This pretty well convinced her Morley was a criminal, and to catch him, she arranged to go to the house as a companion to Miss Grafton. The uncle had been looking out for such a lady, and with Lorraine begging her housekeeper to give Miss Smith (as Kitty christened herself for the role), the position, she was hired on probation, a firm commitment being left to Mr. Morley when he returned from London.

Before leaving next day for London myself, I had a note from Kitty requesting me to make enquiries in the city whether the original Giorgione was known to have been purchased there. This, she felt, would positively incriminate Mr. Morley, though she was already by this time alerted to the name of Uxbridge as a possible criminal. Kitty was very efficient, to give the she-devil her due. She dropped an enticing hint that success in this project might see the Medici door turned over to us at a reasonable price. She had learned as well that Mr. Gwynne, a neighbor not too far away, was believed locally to have the other door. This filled me with excitement. To assemble the whole triptych would be a major coup, and a sort of posthumous fulfilment of my father's futile life as well. He, who loved art so much, would be instrumental in restoring this treasure to mankind.

This was all I knew of Kitty's late history. I went to London, learned after four days close investigation not only who had the original Giorgione portrait, but what he had paid for it, where he had acquired it (from Mr. Uxbridge, of course). To clinch the matter, I got a letter from him stating these facts, which I was to hand over to Mr. Morley, thus positively confirming Uxbridge as a villain. Morley's own part in the affair was unclear, but, of course, the actual working law of Christian ethics is that we are all guilty till proven innocent. In any case, he had proved himself incompetent to handle the collection, and the courts must appoint another person for the job. A hope burgeoned within me that Kitty would apply for it, that I would once and for all rid my life of her opprobrious presence. I was giddy with joy at the prospect, willing to give her any ridiculous sum in settlement of her life-tenancy with me.

I remembered setting out from the Mayhews' with the letter in my reticule, spurning the offer of using their carriage as they would have need of it themselves. I remember Dolly's raised brows when I descended the stairs for the trip wearing a rough cape, round bonnet and old shoes, with matching gown of unbecoming cut beneath.

"I borrowed them of your housekeeper," I told her, laughing. "A disguise, you see, to fool Mr. Gwynne I am not rich. A trick I learned of Kitty. She never wears jewels or furs when she goes to haggle for a painting. She claims it raises the price to learn it is a museum after it, and I daresay she is right. She always strikes an excellent bargain, in any case."

"He'll never believe you could afford a lithograph, let alone an Italian masterpiece," Dolly Mayhew pointed out.

"My conversation is to convince him I am extraordinarily *genteel*, love, but my limited means are all spent on my passion—art. He'll believe the color of my money right enough," I replied, showing her the roll of bills I had got at the bank.

"You shouldn't carry such a sum about with you, Beth," Mr. Mayhew cautioned.

"Pooh, rolled up in a handkerchief in the bottom of my reticule, who is to know it? My poor appearance must divert suspicion that I carry a small fortune on me."

They drove me to the stage, saw me off, and I settled in to enjoy my masquerade. The first move I made once we were moving was to remove the wedding ring from my finger and put it in the capacious pocket of the cape. I would go to Mr. Gwynne as a Miss Mayhew, borrowing a name from my hosts, who were in fact active in a small way in the art world. I did not in the least mind traveling without a companion. My peregrinations across Europe with Papa had robbed me of foolish fears, which Kitty chose to call a sense of propriety. It was a long, dull trip. Leaving in the afternoon, I was not due to reach Gillingham till the next evening, after a sleep-over at Guildford, which we reached after dark the first day of travel. I expected to travel in a style befitting my station, not my cape, an expectation in which I was sorely out. A private parlor was not available for a young lady traveling unchaperoned and plainly outfitted. I had dinner in the common room, jostling elbows with a red-faced cit who would have picked me up for the night if I had not given him a few sharp setdowns. The next indignity was worse by far.

I was to share a room with a woman, (and I don't mean *lady*). With a storm threatening, though not yet broken in full force, there were more people putting up for the night than expected, and there was no private room available for me. In the worst days of traveling with Papa I had not sunk to this, but I was soon given to understand the alternative was to take to the streets at nine-thirty alone, to seek another bed if I declined this offer, so I took the room, to be shared with Miss Weir—either an actress, or worse. She had a painted face and used vulgar, at times even profane, language. She shared my table as well, coming to terms with the cit very early on in the proceedings. Early enough that he picked up her bill, and she ate like a horse.

Sleep was difficult in the unaired chamber with unaired bed, but at least Miss Weir had still not entered when I finally dozed off at some time after midnight. It began to seem I was to have the room to myself after all, with Miss Weir sharing the cit's. It suited me fine. She did come in at some time during the night, however, for in the morning her bleached hair was seen strewn over the pillow across the room from me. My roll of money I had under my pillow. The first thing I did was to check for it, and it was all there. I was not sure, though I suspected, she watched from under her eyelids as I counted it. Now, of course, I know fully well she watched, and my hunch that she had rifled my reticule was also likely accurate. She had left open the little kidskin bag in which I carried powder and hairpins and comb.

Miss Weir loaded on to the stage in the morning, though she had not been on from London. She was at pains to take a seat by me, and I at pains to keep my reticule on the side farther from her, though to tell the truth the person on my other side, a rough-looking man who fancied himself a Lothario, was not much better. What uncouth types one meets on the public conveyances! I had grown out of the custom of such low means of getting around since marrying John.

We lost a wheel at Winchester. The weather was worsening, snow flying and a wind rising. There was some talk of stopping the coach, but while we had dinner the wheel was fixed and it set out again to continue to Salisbury. The road was open that far, and it was said we might have to stop the night there. I had decided to hire a private chaise and go on to Gillingham the next morning in that. We passed through a little place called Wickey, a mere dot on the map with no buildings of any particular interest, but a rather pretty little church tucked in at the corner of the main street. I was happy to see Miss Weir descend from the stage five miles out of Wickey. I was nervous the whole time she was there beside me, trying to make talk, and smelling so strongly of a cheap scent. The Lothario on my other side also descended, leaving me a whole banquette to myself. The coach coming from the west was also stopped a little farther ahead, with some passenger crawling down into the storm. Some local farmer who would have to walk some distance through fields to his home I supposed. I lounged in the corner, trying to get comfortable enough to have a nap, but still making sure I had my reticule tucked against my side. There was a man across from me who looked no better than he should be. I noticed the catch was undone, and did it up quickly. Some little uneasiness was always with me, carrying so much money in cash, and I checked the bottom of my reticule once more to ensure its safety. To my utter horror, the handkerchief was gone! In a flash I knew who had stolen it. Not Miss Weir after all, but Lothario. Her accomplice certainly, though they had been careful not to be seen talking together. *He* I had not suspected of anything but flirting, and he had managed to get into my reticule while she distracted me with her chatter. They had been off the coach for about fifteen minutes, but in the snow we were making poor time, and I thought we had not covered more than a mile. I immediately ordered the coach to be stopped. I hopped down and ran after them, back towards that little place called Wickey.

I was angry as a hornet at having been duped by the pair, wondering how I would catch them. They were likely at the inn, drinking up my money. I would go to the constable's office and have him arrest them. I could describe the handkerchief in which the money was wrapped, with my initial worked by myself, knew exactly the denomination of the bills, too. I regretted I wore such an unimpressive outfit, but meant to succeed despite it. I hurried through the cold night, my anger keeping me not only warm but hot. I suppose they must have been craftier than I thought. Must have lingered along the roadside in case I discovered my loss early on, and waited to assail me. This seemed at first unwise behavior, surely making a bolt was their best bet, but as I considered it, I decided it was greed that led them to their course. Since I kept a close enough eye on my reticule, they knew I would miss the money soon and go after them. I had a rather fine watch pinned to my gown, and carried a chased silver pillbox with stones inset bought by John in France, and a few elegant trifles worth some money. They might have been led to believe from Miss Weir's rifling of my purse that the straw case I carried held more treasures. Actually it had only a change of undergarments and a decent gown and shoes, which I had planned to put on as soon as I had got Gwynne's painting at a good price. In any event, they were waiting for me, hiding behind a tree to leap out on me, silently as shadows, as I hurried past. I think it was the man who actually hit my head with some hard object, while the girl grabbed my reticule and straw bag from my hands. When I came to, lying in the ditch under the tree, the watch was gone, too. Nothing was left me but my clothing, not even my memory.

I had it back now clearly enough. The gaps in my story were due to Kitty's involvement at Grafton's. The fear was a trace of the horror I felt when I saw them appear out of the black night, and the anger was at losing the money, maybe at losing the memory, too, at such a crucial point. What had happened to Kitty and Miss Grafton? Kitty, no shrinking violet, had obviously made sufficient waves that Uxbridge had to get rid of her, but how Miss Grafton came to be likewise stolen away I could not fathom. I *did* know, of course, that Kitty would be wondering why I had not come galloping to her rescue weeks ago, all the while I sojourned merrily at Granhurst. I was likely closer to her now than I had been in all that time. My kidnapper was Uxbridge, obviously. Oh yes, a little undistinguished man who would never stand out in any crowd! Funny that description had not struck me as pertinent, but then he had acted his part so well, feigning reluctance to have me with him when he must have known all the time I was in desperate straits, friendless, alone, running. Must have followed me—us—from Granhurst to the Bay House, and been awaiting a chance to get at me.

Did Sir Ludwig know it, and was that why I had been held a virtual prisoner? But still I could conceive of no reason why he should have turned against me. I was guilty of no more than attempting to get a good price for my missing madonna from Mr. Gwynne—a standard business procedure. What did he think I had done, that he should condemn me as a bitch and threaten me with ten years in prison? Something worse than wear a poor cape when I could have afforded a better, surely. I puzzled over this for several moments, trying to see where he went wrong. He knew I was Mrs. Knightsbridge—had called me so in a manner that was not hesitant or reluctant. He knew. Knew who I was, then, but not what I was. He still thought it possible I was involved in the kidnapping and double-dealing of Uxbridge. He must have thought I was running *to* Uxbridge—that I was the man's accomplice. I could think of no better reason.

If he succeeded in following my trail, he would be certain of it, going with Uxbridge to Wight. Certain, too, to follow us, I thought with a wave of relief. How long would it be likely to take? Where he had dashed off to the night before I had no idea, unless it were back to Morley for some help in the ransom business. I tried to struggle out of my bonds, rough prickly cords that scratched my wrists and ankles. They were very securely tied, indeed. I wiggled my hands about till my wrists were raw, and still hadn't loosened the knots perceptibly.

Dawn was filtering through the dusty partitioned window. The navy blue rectangles became indigo, pearl gray, settling in to a dirty white eventually. It was going to be that kind of a day. I was thoroughly chilled, my muscles cramped, my stomach empty and growling, my head thumping, and most of all my temper was exacerbated with frustration at my helplessness. Why did no one come to give me food? Did he plan to starve me to death? Had he done the same to Kitty and Miss Grafton? Or were they in this same building with me, locked in some other chamber? He would not have his victims scattered around the countryside, involving various keepers. No, we—if we were all still alive—had been spirited to this quiet, out-of-the-way little island, off the beaten track. An excellent prison really, but I fancied the prison that could long hold me was yet to be built.

Chapter Sixteen

It was somewhere close to noon before a slovenly dame unlocked my door and placed a mess of potage on the floor in a cracked bowl. By that time I had long since got out of my ropes and had been banging on the floor, walls and shouting through the broken window, all without a single sign of reaction from anyone, I might add. I began firing questions at her, but observed that her surliness was due as much to intoxication as ill humor. She had been swilling gin since breakfast, to judge from the reeking odors coming from her mouth and her haphazard manner of looking around. She did not appear to notice that I had slipped my bindings. Not a helpful word did I get out of her, nor was there anything in the room to use for a weapon. She was so large and rough looking that I didn't quite dare tackle her empty-handed.

Kitty had somewhat better luck, perhaps because Miss Grafton was there to help her. It was about an hour later that I heard a soft tapping at the door. I had no notion of replying, as I thought it would be my jaileress, and I preferred her to open the door to ascertain I was still within, on the off chance that I might manage to fell her. The bowl of potage, still on the floor, was a possible club. I was hungry, but not quite that hungry. The taps were soon followed by whispered words. "Beth—Beth, is it you?"

Who would ever have thought I would be happy to hear Kitty Empey's voice? But I was. I bounded to the locked door and began shouting excited questions to her.

"Hush! Be still—you'll be heard," she said, very much in her old domineering way. "We'll try to get the door open. Lorraine has a key she took from another chamber door. It might fit." There were already the clicking sounds of this expedient being tried, and before long the door opened with a squeak. Kitty and a young girl dressed in black stepped in, the former looking very much like herself, except that her gown was the worse for wear, and her complexion had either suffered or she had been wearing rouge for the past several years. This latter was by no means impossible. I had often suspected it.

"Well, what have you to say for yourself?" was her first remark upon seeing me in what I am convinced was a worse predicament than her own. The indignities of the past day must have been evident on my person.

I was too relieved to reply in kind. I threw my arms around the old witch and hugged her, placing a kiss smack on her mole. She disentangled herself brusquely and pushed me away.

"You must be Miss Grafton," I said to the other, a pretty, bright-eyed young lady, greatly disheveled, with jam stains all down the front of her gown—or some messy substance, anyway.

Kitty performed very solemn introductions, as though we were in a polite saloon. With a commanding look to

Miss Grafton, Kitty nudged her forward to perform a curtsy.

"Now then," Kitty said, the important preliminary over with, "I expect our first business is to escape. We aren't likely to have such a chance again. Dobble has gone with Uxbridge somewhere, and only the slattern is here protecting us. She was three sheets to the wind when she brought lunch, and is likely completely insensate by now. At least she didn't come running when we broke through the panel of the door. Fortunately our door was one of those cheap ones with a thin panel inset, and by bumping it with the end of Lorraine's bed, we managed to break through it. I heard you screech to wake the dead, Beth."

Funny I hadn't heard them, but I had no idea of the size of the house, nor its construction. "Gather up your things and let us be off," she commanded next.

There was nothing to gather except my bonnet. My cape and shoes were on me for warmth. My gloves lost somewhere. We went together down the attic stairs, along a long, dark hallway to the far end of the house, past about eight bedrooms, to get their cloaks and bonnets, then ventured, one behind the other, Kitty in the lead, down the main stairs to the ground floor. All was silent. The front door was locked, but from the inside with a sliding bolt. We went out, made a dash down the stairs, down the driveway, into a complete wilderness. The house was a summer home, set on the banks of a creek that was probably honored with the name river. There wasn't a single sign of human life anywhere around us, but there were carriage tracks, leading to a road we assumed. We took off down it as if our lives depended on it, as they did for all I know. We were considerably frightened of meeting a carriage coming up the road, and a carriage on this road could lead to nowhere but our prison. We met no vehicle of any sort before reaching the main road about a mile farther on.

Kitty, who has the nerve for anything, hailed up the first decent looking coach that passed and talked our way into it. She wore her good fur-lined pelisse and her hat had withstood the ravages of incarceration better than my own or Miss Grafton's. With her high-handed manner, she got us all taken into Newport, which happened to be where the gentleman was going.

I thought it would be the constable's office we headed to, but Kitty said the inn, and it was to the inn that we went. I had recovered sufficiently to be wondering how we should pay for this luxury, but knew Kitty would manage somehow. She ordered up a private parlor and a bottle of wine. She then turned on me with the wrath of Jehovah to demand an accounting of my part in 'this infamous affair' as it was henceforth known in her interminable accounts of it. "I'll stay away from the police till I hear what you have been up to," she informed me. "I have no desire to have John's name dragged through the mud."

After all we had been through, she hadn't changed a whit. She was still Kitty, determined to rule me and the world with an iron hand. She had not been tardy to get Miss Grafton under her thumb, I noticed. She *did* treat the girl more gently than she ever treated me, but it was a gentle tyranny, nothing else. It was Lorraine's possession of persons lofty enough to be termed 'ancestors' that accounted for it. There was an earl lurking somewhere there on the mother's side of the family tree, it turned out. My own predecessors were not mighty enough for her, featuring numerous army officers and the like on Papa's side. Somewhat better on my mother's, but I took after Papa.

"So you forgot all about us once you got off to London with those rackety Mayhewses," she suggested, delighted to think she had the whip in her hand.

I told my story, of which she believed less than a tenth, I think. But for the fact that I ended up in that attic, even one tenth would not have been credited.

The telling was interrupted by a million questions.

"How does it come the Mayhewses have not been enquiring for you?" she demanded.

"I told them I would stay as long as it took to get the matter concluded."

"They can't have thought it would take a *month!*"

"They probably *have* been enquiring. They would not have thought of enquiring at Wickey, however."

"Who is this Sir Ludwig you speak of? I never heard of him. Sounds like a foreigner to me. Does your family know him, Lorraine?"

She shook her head in a negative. "Nobody in other words, and you putting up a month with a bachelor. Upon my word, I don't know what the bishop will have to say of this."

A request to hear her side of the infamous affair diverted her tirade. She was dying to get it licked into a shape that featured her as a heroine. A few details changed over later tellings, but this is the gist of it, as it first came from her lips. Lorraine was not allowed to say a word except an occasional corroboration of a minor detail.

"I gathered details of mismanagement of the Grafton's estate—you know about the sales and forgery," she began *in media res*, the beginning familiar to us all. "My first plan of broaching my information to Morley awaited his return, but when Uxbridge came as bold as you please to snatch another painting from the wall for selling, I forbade it. He had got a piece of paper from that *idiot* Morley giving him permission, *carte blanche*, to do whatever he wished with the collection. So I had to tell him who I am," she announced, as though she were a queen at least. "I told him quite frankly I meant to call in a magistrate to look into the infamous dealings he had engineered on behalf of the estate. He said, 'Go ahead,' bold as you please, but I could see he was shaken. He later that same day sent me a note requesting me to go to his home, only in Shaftesbury, you know, a few miles away, and we would 'work out a satisfactory solution.' I thought he meant to return the money he had stolen in exchange for my not pressing charges, as if I would be put off so easily! But that was not his meaning at all. Nothing of the sort. The rogue implied, when I got there, that I was to receive a share of the profits. That was his original intention, to silence me with money. I was never so insulted in my life. He had a very wrong idea of my character, and so I told him. *Then* what did the bold man do but threaten me. He meant to be rid of me before Mr. Morley got home—kill me, or do I hardly know what. He trussed me up in ropes and threw me into the cellar. Such a filthy hole I never saw in my life! But Lorraine," she smiled benignly on this rich possessor of ancestors, "had come with me. He didn't know that. She had gone on to the shops in Shaftesbury for half an hour and was to pick me up after at Uxbridge's place. He found himself at *point non plus* when Lorraine landed at his door asking for me. He hadn't intended harming her, for he knew she was too highly placed in Society, cousin to Lord Baxford—an earl. He tried to be rid of her, but she sensed something wrong and refused to leave. Indeed I had been a little leary of going alone, and mentioned it to her, as a precaution. Not that I had thought he would sink to outright violence with a lady. Lorraine stood firm and refused to leave. When she began to threaten having in the police, there was nothing for it but to chuck her into the cellar as well. I don't know what he thought to do with us, and neither, I think, did he. He took on a good deal more than he bargained for, without knowing it. Lord Baxford would see to his destruction if *other people* did not consider it worth their while." Need I say, the *other people* were myself?

"He realized, I suppose, that he would be the first one to fall under suspicion, and got us packed out of his house in the middle of the night, both drugged. He put the stuff in coffee, just as he did with you, Beth. It was the only bite we had all that day, and we were hungry and thirsty enough to drink it. I'll never take coffee again unless I see it poured into my cup with my own eyes. We hadn't a notion where we were. I never knew, all these days, we were on a small island—had no idea we had crossed water at all. He gave us a dose large enough to knock out a horse. It's a mercy we weren't both dead. We have been treated perfectly wretchedly. I haven't been out of my clothes since the day we were abducted, the first of December, and it is now—well, I've lost track of when it is, but I suppose it must be January."

"January the sixth."

"Hardly more than a month—it seems years. I'm sure this gown could stand up and walk by itself. And yours too, Lorraine. A dozen times a day I asked him what he meant to do, and threatened him with all sorts of horrid reprisals if he touched us, and all the time I was waiting for *you* to come and rescue us. But it is exactly like you to go losing your memory at such a time. I never heard of anyone else ever doing such a thing. It is very odd, too, that Morely made no efforts to find us. I'm not half convinced he is innocent."

I mentioned Morley's assorted efforts, which she whisked aside as nothing with one bat of her hands. "The man is an imbecile, if not worse. The only thing that inclines me to believe him innocent is his stupidity." All this without having thus far made his acquaintance.

"I wonder how Uxbridge tumbled to it *I* was involved in the affair? It must be he who attacked me at the chapel." Thus far, I saw no way in which he could know it.

"I told him," she informed me. "Threatened him a dozen times that Mrs. Knightsbridge, widow of Mr. John Knightsbridge of the Knightsbridge Museum in Edinburgh was my niece-in-law, and would be looking for me. He must have pieced two and two together and figured out who you were when Morley spoke of having met you at this Gwynne person's home. Uxbridge left us in the Dobbles' keeping for weeks at a stretch. He was away more often than he was here, but we had no way of knowing what he was about. He was afraid you'd suddenly remember who you were, and come looking for us. I told him you were well aware of all his goings-on, and were in fact at that very moment in London documenting his forgery of the Giorgione. I daresay he couldn't believe his luck that you had lost your memory, but he would want to get ahold of you in case it came back to you. You were a positive menace to him."

"Did you know he sent a ransom note in your name? Miss Smith's name, I mean?"

"It was my own idea," she answered, smiling triumphantly. "*He* didn't know what to do with us. We could have died of boredom in that ramshackle house with the Dobbles browbeating us if *I* hadn't taken a hand in it. The idea of getting a good sum for us pleased him, and it pleased me that he was getting more deeply into crime. The law would take kidnapping more seriously than a disappearance. Then too, the delivery of the money I hoped he might mismanage in a way that could lead the police to us. I even told him a sum that could be easily raised, so that Morley would get on with it at once. Ten thousand?" she verified.

"Exactly."

"I didn't realize he had put my name on it. Forgery—there is another crime to his list. If he doesn't hang for this there is no justice in the land."

Somehow, I was beginning to entertain a sliver of pity for Mr. Uxbridge.

"For all we know, it may have been the idea of ransom money that led him to kidnap you in the end. *You* didn't know who you were, but I knew, and gave him a slightly exaggerated idea of your worth, to make him treat us with respect. Yes, as he was dipping a toe into kidnapping and ransom, he probably thought he might as well get something for you while he was about it. I daresay that jackdandy Soames you hired to handle the museum while we were away hasn't done a thing in Edinburgh, after not hearing from us in a month. And I *told* him I would be in touch at least once a week. You might *much* better have left it in Ivor's hands."

The last name caused a face to pop into my head, and a feeling of revulsion. Ivor Knightsbridge, John's nephew (thirty-eight), who stood to inherit the whole if I married, but as I had made no move to do so, he was trying his hand at courting me himself. Not that he cared for me at all. He would infinitely prefer I marry someone else. I was too forward to please him. He alternately dangled after me and urged me on Mr. Soames, a highly romantical young fellow lately graduated from Oxford, and looking about for a career for himself. The fact of my being rich and in a position to give up a good piece of the world for him appeals to his sense of the dramatic. He quite regularly suggested an elopement, but as he hasn't a feather to fly with, nor would I have if I succumbed to his petitions, we only carried on an *à suivre* flirtation, vastly annoying to the relatives. They all worry about my petticoats, not only Ivor.

"I wonder what he meant to do after he got the money," I said.

"Go to France," she answered readily. "I convinced him he would be safe there, and with the ten thousand pounds he could have a very comfortable sort of existence. I had to make him believe he would get away safely, or he'd have taken into his head to *kill* us after he got the money. I convinced him British justice would let a kidnapper off, but cross the sea to apprehend a murderer. I daresay there is a grain of truth in it. He thought so in any case."

I don't like Kitty. I have to try very hard not to hate her at times, but I grant her a begrudging respect, bordering even on admiration. Poor Mr. Uxbridge went beyond his depths when he tangled with that vixen.

With our story all sorted out in a manner that freed me of criminal prosecution, Kitty was ready to call in the law. She strode to the doorway of the parlor to open it and call a servant, just as two gentlemen came pelting into the hallway. It was Sir Ludwig and Mr. Williker. I wonder what she thought when I ran forward and threw myself into Ludwig's arms. No better than she expected of me, I daresay.

Chapter Seventeen

I forgot in my first joy of seeing Ludwig that he thought me a reprobate. I think he forgot it, too, for Kitty was treated to the view of a quite abandoned embrace, which fueled her lectures for the next several weeks. She was soon into the hallway, pulling us bodily apart from each other, and enjoining me to some semblance of behavior, if I could 'control my lust' till I was alone with my 'paramour.' I can't think what it was she read that gave her such a vivid vocabulary. The only books ever seen in her possession were of the most edifying and sanctimonious, usually recommended by her relative, the bishop.

Ludwig was glowering at me even while he clutched at my hands, wishing, I know, to demand an explanation and berate me, but put off by my woeful appearance and the total lack of abasement that would naturally follow the sort of behavior he imputed to me. To hide our shame from the onlookers who were gathering in open doorways, Kitty hustled us into the private parlor and closed the door, with a hard stare at those ill-bred enough to try to overhear matters that were none of their concern.

"And *this,* I take it," she said with a sneer to Kessler, "is the *person* with whom you have been living since you say you lost your memory."

"Who the devil is she?" he asked, in much the same voice.

"Kitty," I told him, and giggled in mingled relief and appreciation of our mutual predicament.

"Good Lord, you mean there really is a Kitty?" he asked.

"I, sir, am Miss Catherine Empey, aunt to the late John Knightsbridge of the Knightsbridge Museum in Edinburgh," she explained.

"Oh, Miss Smith," he remarked, nodding and honoring her with only the minutest of a glance.

There followed a long and confused period of explanations, with everyone interrupting and correcting everyone else except Lorraine Grafton, who just looked, and occasionally nodded her approval of Kitty's recital of the infamous affair. Having heard it once already, I listened closely for those rare occasions when Ludwig got a word in over Kitty's head. When she turned to Mr. Williker to start in on the utter lack of help Bow Street had been in the business, I got Ludwig aside to demand why he had chosen to describe me as a bitch, and why I had been summarily tossed into the attic of Bay House.

I received not a single word of apology, but a very brief account of the reason, which I felt *did* deserve an apology as he had knowingly subjected me to danger.

"After you took to your bed that day Morley called, he came back with a detail he'd forgotten to mention, a letter for Mrs. Knightsbridge from London. The clunch hadn't the sense to open it, but we tore it open then and discovered some people from London called Mayhew were worried that you had not returned to them. It was pretty clear then that Miss Empey was at the Graftons' under an alias, and that you were to go to her. After the attack in the park and seeing Uxbridge skulking around Wickey again—Miss Wickey pointed him out to me as the man who had asked for you at the rectory—I figured he was after you. We first planned to sit tight at Granhurst and wait for the demand for ransom money, hoping to catch him that way, but the note, received later that same day, asked for the money to be deposited in a bank account in Paris, and this made capture so difficult and delayed that I came up with another plan.

"Uxbridge seemed reluctant to come after you at Granhurst, so I decided to let him see you were leaving, going to a nice isolated spot. He was watching, of course, and saw us leave for Bay House. It was the plan that he would try to get to you there, and Peters and myself, hiding in the stable, were to catch him. It threw me for a loss when you went out after him. Why the devil did you?"

"I wasn't going after *him*! I thought I was a kidnapper, and only wanted to run away and hide somewhere. And if you knew who I was, you might have told me and set my mind at rest."

"I wanted to, Rose. Especially in the carriage I wanted to, but Fell thought the best way was to let you remember for yourself. He felt it would be too confusing to just try to tell you—it would delay your recovery even more."

"And what if Uxbridge had decided to *kill* me while he had the chance?"

"He wouldn't have had the chance. You were guarded better than a diamond. There was some doubt as well, that first day and night, as to Mrs. Knightsbridge's *total* innocence in the affair. Williker told me it is said in Edinburgh that Mrs. Knightsbridge chaffed under the shackles of polite society. Her fortune being tied up so tightly led her relatives to believe she was trying her hand at getting some cash to enable her to marry a certain Mr. Soames, who sounds a proper jackdaw, I must say."

"They would think that! And on the word of a pack of total strangers you took into your head to believe me a criminal?"

"That combined with the fact that you were running away. And I still don't understand why you *were* running. Just where did you plan to go, without a penny in your pockets?"

"Why, to some bachelor's establishment, of course! What did you think?"

"Well, to tell the truth, Rose, when your eyes grew an inch at the sight of Mrs. Knightsbridge's handwriting, and when Abbie told me yours was the same, I suspected you might have gone astray a little. Oh I don't mean I thought you had disposed of Kitty and Miss Grafton—though really, now I have met Kitty . . . I only meant I thought maybe you had picked up a family necklace or some such thing and bolted. I didn't blame you."

"So you went back to Granhurst that first night, did you?"

"Lord no, I told you I hid in the stables at Bay House. I sent a groom from Bay House back to find out what was going on, and he had Williker come along to me. I only went back the next day, after I had you locked in the attic. And I don't know why I did even then, except Williker kept chattering about the ransom. We turned around and came back almost as soon as we got there, only to find you gone. Peters had discovered you went to Wight, and at Hythe we learned that our mysterious, insignificant-looking gent had joined you, and from there it was follow the hare, to enquire after Mr. Colroy, the name he used on the mainland. No relation to the real Colroy, of course, who will very likely press charges of his own for using his name in vain."

"Have you still not caught Uxbridge, then?"

"You haven't kept your eyes open, Rose. Williker

skipped out the door five minutes ago, headed for Uxbridge's place. He will go back there to check on his various prisoners sooner or later—Uxbridge. Bow Street will be waiting for him when he does."

"Shouldn't someone have gone with him? Dobble will be there, too, I suppose."

"Williker mentioned picking up a constable at the station here before leaving. He has a gun, anyway, and could probably handle a pair of them alone. We don't know exactly where Uxbridge is at the moment. He followed us to Bay House and obviously hung around there till he met up with you by lucky chance. I suppose that as Peters and I guarded you so well, he meant to desert you, and skip to France on his profits from his other two ladies. He might be out booking passage now, but he'll go back to that house first, don't you think?"

"I suppose so. Dobble's wife is there, so they must plan to return."

Out of the corner of my eye I noticed often that Kitty was looking at me, and soon after Williker left, she interrupted my tête-à-tête with Ludwig to begin making plans for returning to the mainland. We none of us wished to go in our filthy rags, and with our stomachs empty.

"Have you plenty of money with you?" she asked Ludwig, her tone implying she doubted he had any, either with him or anywhere else.

"Just put it on my bill," I told him aside.

He took out a reassuringly heavy purse. With this to go on, we hired a pair of rooms. I was told by Kitty I was to go out and purchase clean clothing for herself and Lorraine Grafton. The quality was not important, providing it was clean and decent. I nodded obligingly to be rid of her, but it was a serving girl at the inn who performed the errand while I tidied my own appearance in the other room, finishing up two hours before herself and Lorraine, who had a month's scrubbing before them. Then I joined Ludwig below for a private dinner in our parlor, a trick that primed Kitty for an hour's rant when she discovered it. Any little points that bothered either Ludwig or myself were explained in detail, along with some of my ancient history, that period preceding John and Italy.

"So, now you know exactly who I am, Ludwig, and you can stop calling me Rose Trelawney and Miss Smith. And *I* can write you a check for all the money you were kind enough to loan me."

"Better attend to it, before your fortune is cut down to a hundred pounds, eh?" was the only hint I received as to my future.

By the time Kitty and Lorraine descended, the hour was so far advanced that we decided to go no farther than Bay House that night. We were all anxious to get off the island. Lud managed to get ahold of a boat, and not long after nightfall we were at Bay House. The next morning we went on home, in Ludwig's traveling carriage.

Kitty was determined I should go to the Grafton's with her, and I equally determined I would not. We took her and Lorraine to Gillingham, and I went on to Granhurst.

"I hope you can talk him into marrying you," was her parting shot, delivered in a voice loud enough to be overheard, low enough to pretend it was for my ears alone. "You have certainly managed to ruin your reputation, otherwise."

"You hear that?" I asked him as we closed the door behind us and went to the carriage to continue our journey.

"Certainly puts me in the driver's seat," he informed me. "I shall draw up a list of my conditions for marrying a penniless widow of unsavory reputation and managing disposition."

"And expensive tastes! That grass rug in the morning parlor . . ."

"Very expensive tastes," he agreed. "I shall work out my list and let you know."

"Don't make it too stringent. You will remember Mr. Soames and Ivor Knightsbridge waiting for me at home. And I won't be quite penniless after paying you my hundred pounds either, for I have Papa's piece of the triptych."

"Its sale might re-cover the morning parlor floor," he suggested.

"Ludwig, I shan't sell it! You must try to get the other pieces from Gwynne and Miss Grafton."

"Well now, it seems to me you are rushing things. You haven't talked me into having *you*, yet. I am looking forward to the conversation. Start talking, Rose," he said, and immediately began the conversation by pulling me into his arms and kissing me so hard my lips hurt. We discussed the matter in this fashion the better part of the way to Granhurst, and by the time we arrived, I seemed to have talked him into it. He was devising schemes to help me get the two triptych doors in any case, while I implanted in his head the notion that his chapel, still unseen by me, would be a suitable repository for this religious artwork.

Annie and Abigail were at their wits' end to hear what had happened. They both looked heartily relieved to see us enter arm-in-arm, laughing and talking.

"Well, and is she a crook or ain't she?" was Annie's happy salutation.

"Sorry, Cousin, no," Ludwig told her. "Only a very devious woman."

"Ho, I know very well she's *that*," Annie replied, "Damme, but I hoped you'd be a *real* criminal," she added to me, a little wistfully. "And you never stole a thing then, nor kidnapped the little Grafton girl or browbeat Miss Smith into disguising herself?"

"No, Annie, but I have been poisoned and tied up and subjected to the greatest of indignities."

"Oh Rose Trelawney!" she beamed. "Was you raped?"

"I don't believe so," I answered.

"I'll bet you were. The very reason he doped you, I daresay. The villain. You want to break his nose, Lud."

"I'll be sure to do that."

"Have you got any bumps to show us?" Annie pressed on.

"My wrists are all raw from the ropes," I mentioned, for they were stinging, "but I have no bumps this time."

She came to admire my red wrists, with the rest of the family following suit. "Get some bandages and medications, Abbie," Ludwig said curtly. "Why didn't you have Mrs. Peters attend to this last night?" he asked me angrily, but I was not deceived by this Germanic outburst. It was Uxbridge he wanted to shout at.

While I rubbed salve into my wrists, Ludwig sat by telling me I wasn't using enough and voicing sundry complaints. Abbie looked on, then asked, "Now are we to hear the climax of the story?"

"That's about it," her brother told her. "Unless you refer to the clean-up of the affair when Williker captures Uxbridge."

"But what is Mrs. Knightsbridge to do? Is she returning to Scotland?"

"No, she is staying with us," he answered. That was our wedding announcement.

"For how long?" Annie asked.

"For good," he said.

"He means till death do us part," I expanded, which was clear to Abbie, who had soon relayed her information to Annie.

"Good. That calls for a drink, then," Annie exclaimed.

"Yes, let us have a cup of tea," Ludwig suggested.

I saw I had my work cut out for me, bringing a sense of style to this motley crew. For that one evening, however, I was too exhausted to assert myself, and settled in with the others for a cup of tea, while Annie rattled on, "That favorite spaniel of yours, Lud, the one that peed on the carpet, has got into your room again and ate up your slippers."

"A pity it hadn't been that old piece of lumber you call a desk. You would be well rid of it," I mentioned, while Ludwig regarded me questioningly.

"I hadn't realized you were planning on redoing my bedchamber," he remarked. "That the plans were already under way, I mean."

Chapter Eighteen

Kitty, Miss Grafton and Mr. Morley descended on us the next morning, almost before we had gulped our breakfast down, for we all arose very late. I was happy to see I was not the only person who knuckled under to her. Mr. Morley clearly went in mortal terror of her tongue, and Miss Grafton treated her as a sort of goddess, which is exactly the way she likes to be treated. It was soon out that she intended battening herself on them, under circumstances slightly altered from my own at Edinburgh.

"Lorraine is *begging* me to stay on," she said, with a sapient eye to me. *Here* I am appreciated, the look said. "Certainly *someone* must be hired to oversee the running of the Grafton collection. Mr. Morley admits quite frankly he doesn't know a thing about art." The word 'hire' was slid in quietly, but it told me she meant to extract a salary for her help. He looked, as usual, worried.

"And Lorraine will be making her come-out next

year," Kitty spoke on. "She will require a respectable female for that job, and as her mother's second cousin once-removed, I am well suited for the post."

That was the only light I perceived in the matter for Miss Grafton. Her position under Kitty's thumb would be brief, if she found a husband that could stand up to the old witch. The collection would be in good hands, however, and as it made up the better part of the girl's fortune, this was no small consideration.

"What are *your* plans, Elizabeth?" she demanded next.

"I plan to marry Sir Ludwig and remain here."

She fairly grinned at this intelligence. Not that she was happy to see me nab a good husband. She would have been infinitely happier to see me make a runaway match with a penniless rake, but my marriage would put the Knightsbridge Museum back in the hands of the Knightsbridges, where she felt, perhaps rightly, it had always belonged. "Ivor will take over in Edinburgh, then," she smiled. The smile was followed closely by a frown. Her staying down south would put her out of close touch with Ivor and the museum, but then Ivor had a mind of his own, and she would play only second fiddle there, while she could be the *maestra* of the whole here. She was already speaking of a trip to London to appeal to the gentlemanly instincts of those who had purchased 'her' pictures, the ones Uxbridge had sold, to see if they could not be recovered.

Kitty still considered myself to be her responsibility, and her next move was to ascertain what sort of a man I was marrying. I was happy I had got the main saloon redone. It gave a good impression, but she was soon disparaging my future home. "Your facade, Sir Ludwig, is a poor copy of Schloss Ludwigsburg, I believe? Something of the main part of the original has been attempted out front, I think?"

He admitted it to be the case, and sat listening while she outlined where the builder had gone wrong. Entablatures were but inferior imitations of the original, the charming little oval window on the third story had been forgotten, statues were missing—in short, the worst had been badly copied while the best was omitted, but in the end she allowed it to be 'a pretty little place, if one cared for that misapplied touch of Baroque on a basically Renaissance building.' For herself, she would rather have a good honest cottage than a botched copy of anything. Ludwig allowed, with a raised brow to her befeathered bonnet, that there was certainly no accounting for taste. *He* had always found it repugnant that ladies reconstructed dead birds to wear on their heads.

She next tried to hint him into a disclosure of what capital and income I was marrying into. "Beth is used to the very best, you must know. That is to say, after she married John she became accustomed to the best. Had her own carriage and team and even a set of small diamonds. They will stay with the estate, of course."

"If my diamonds are too large for her, she is free to buy a smaller set," he replied. "Nor have I any objection to her limiting herself to a single team for her carriages."

Stymied on this score, she rushed in to ascertain what I had not yet got out of Ludwig myself, namely, when the great day was to be.

"That will be up to Rose," he told her.

"Rose who?" she asked, ready to take umbrage, and glancing angrily to Abbie and Annie.

"Rose Trelawney of course," Annie snapped. She had taken Kitty in dislike from the first moment. The dislike had mounted to hatred when Kitty told her she took too much sugar in her tea.

"Who is Rose Trelawney that she has anything to say in the matter?" Kitty demanded, struck nearly speechless at the idea.

Rose was explained, and received with disdain. "I suppose the marriage will take place at once?" she asked knowingly. She might as well have said what she meant. If you don't nab him fast, he'll shab off on you.

"In a few months," I answered, when I wanted to do it as soon as possible.

Ludwig looked surprised, but he was coming to know me well enough to understand my answer, I think. "Perhaps in the summer," he added, with a smile behind her back.

"You never want to wait so long," she cautioned me.

"I rather fancy a fall wedding myself," I said, pushing the date ever farther away.

Abbie said, "Oh, Rose, you won't want to wait so long!"

"Pooh, what's the difference?" Annie scoffed. "They're as good as married already."

Kitty's eyes were in danger of leaving her head. They flew from myself to Ludwig, in joyful condemnation. Annie rattled on, heedless of any indiscretion. "Mind you, Lud, Rose don't care for the way your bedroom looks. She tells me she is not happy with it at all. She will be smartening it up now that she's actually to marry you."

"Yes, when she is *legally* mistress of the place, she may do as she pleases with our bedroom," he answered, stolid as an owl.

"Well upon my word!" Kitty said, and sagged back against her chair. "Lorraine, I think it is time we leave. Until you see fit to legalize your status, Elizabeth, I shall not return to this house."

"There's nothing illegal about Rose Trelawney," Annie defended me. "What does she mean? What is she getting at?" she demanded of us all. "You can't mean the creature thinks you and Lud are carrying on an affair! Well, upon my word! Leave it to an old spinster to think the worst."

Kitty very soon left, but not before another request to be informed of the date. It was put off by Ludwig and myself till it began to seem we would be rolling to the altar in a couple of bathchairs. When at last she was gone, Lud asked calmly, "When shall we actually be married?"

"I'd like a proper wedding, with banns read," I told him. "In Italy it was such a scrambling little do that I'd like to have a larger ceremony this time."

"I'll have the banns started next Sunday, then," he answered.

Abbie looked at us as though we were mad. "Hadn't you better tell Miss Empey?" she asked.

"Oh no, she will take over the whole if she knows. I'll send her a card, but not till the last minute," I answered.

A card could not actually be held off till the very last minute, of course, and as soon as it was received, Kitty took the dreadful habit of dropping in every third or fourth day to check on the progress of the nuptials. "Of course you will go to Edinburgh for your honeymoon," she told me.

This appalling idea sent Ludwig into a state of shock. It is only natural a husband not wish to return to the wife's first home on his wedding trip, but really there was some merit in the suggestion. I had all my personal belongings to be gathered and brought south. I had, most of all, my share of the triptych I wished to get. A compromise was struck between us. We were to go to London for our wedding trip, which would put me back in touch with my wardrobe at Mayhews, and at an early date were to go to Scotland to wind up affairs there.

Before either the wedding or any trip, Mr. Uxbridge was apprehended by Mr. Williker on Wight, where he *did* go to oversee all his prisoners. He and the Dobbles were turned over to the authorities for punishment. They all escaped the noose, to Kitty's consternation. But then it was a fitting climax to the 'infamous affair' that the culprits get off scot free, as she termed twenty years in prison. We learned the actual sentence from the McCurdles in Wickey. They always knew everything, sometimes before it happened. Kitty, as I might have foreseen had I given the matter any thought, struck up a wonderful friendship with this pair of harpies, who filled her head with all manner of evil doings on my part, while she filled them in on my earlier history. My torturing of the schoolboys at the rectory, refusal to take up a *decent* home with themselves, preferring to pitch my cap at the neighborhood's richest bachelor, my lazy way of going on while with Miss Wickey, my constant running to the shops to order up new gowns, all was magnified out of all proportion to Kitty, till I had the very character Kitty always wanted me to have. She could learn no ill of Ludwig except that he was the most gullible of the works of God to have been taken in by me. Her last visit sunk to a weary hour of her shaking her head sadly at him, eyes full of pity for his bleak future with a trollop.

The wedding went forth on the announced date, followed by the trip to London. We had a perfectly marvelous time, with not more than half a dozen fights a day, always concluded in the time-honored manner of kissing and making up. I expect I was a perfectly wretched wife to John, who was too easy to bearlead. I shall deal much better with Ludwig. He is the sort who would turn into a domestic tyrant if he were allowed. He wants a wife who will give him a little opposition. He has acquired one who will give him a great deal. Being rid of the hunter-green drapes and salmon carpet is by no means the end of my plans for Granhurst. There is the matter of the bedroom awaiting my talents. I refer to decor. And there is the grass rug, and the dull food placed on the table. Plenty to keep me busy.

Lud was difficult to get moving once we were back at Granhurst. It was necessary for me to point out his company was not really necessary in the least, for once I was there, either Ivor or Mr. Soames would be delighted to squire me about Scotland. It was actually the visit of Lord Baxford which got us shot off without being at all prepared for the trip. He was visiting Lorraine at the Graftons', and Kitty brought him over to show him off to us. He took into his head to be rolling his eyes at me, silly old fool. I only encouraged him to make Kitty jealous, but when he mentioned coming back the next day, Ludwig suddenly decided we were leaving for Scotland early the next morning.

What should happen but that Kitty took the abominable idea of dragging Miss Grafton up north to see the Knightsbridge Museum as a part of her artistic education. Did it while we were there, but it could not be helped. Her real aim was to promote a match between Ivor and Lorraine while the girl was young and foolish, but the scheme did not take. It was Soames that caught the girl's eye, and vice versa. In the end, Kitty left a good deal sooner than she had intended, to separate them. We stayed not a moment longer than necessary, just long enough to gather up my belongings and sign some papers. I didn't get the hundred pounds. They said I had been overdrawn on my allowance, having taken an advance to finance the trip south. In fact, I owed them fifty pounds, and I now owe Ludwig fifty more.

Ivor was alerted by Kitty to keep a sharp eye on my packing, lest I pack up any *bibelots* that did not belong to me. I didn't, but Ludwig was so incensed at their scrutiny that he pocketed a pretty little Renaissance inkwell in spite, and threw it out of the window of the carriage into a ditch before we made our first stop, as I convinced him Ivor would have the constable after us. We were back at Granhurst before we heard anything else about it, in a letter from Ivor. I declined to reply at all, but Kitty, I am sure, relayed my ire at the suggestion.

So I am now settled in comfortably at Granhurst, known in the village as Lady Kessler, a female of shady background, but tolerated because of my husband. I am still in a rant occasionally when I meet opposition at home to my renovations. We are busy as bees pulling down curtains and up carpets. We have quit pretending to look for either a governess or school for Abbie. We will not part with her, and a strange female around the house bothers Ludwig. Kitty managed by some unknown means to get the missing madonna out of Gwynne for *her* collection. He speaks highly of her, and has twice had her and Morley and Lorraine to dinner, along with ourselves. Thus far the invitation has not been returned, but one day I wouldn't be surprised to see Kitty overseeing yet a different collection of paintings. I hope not, as Gwynne's place is so close to our own.

She got the madonna from him while we were in London. The romance had not yet blossomed at that time, and I don't know what price he extracted for it, but if she thinks she will now get the other piece from me, she is mad as a hatter. I wouldn't let her have it for a million pounds. I didn't put it in the chapel after all, as it was too damp and draughty. It sits in the blue Saloon, to annoy Kitty every time she drops in.

After her last visit, Ludwig turned to me with a consoling smile. "I know now why you were so eager to forget your past," he told me. "It must have been hell, under that cat's paw from dawn to dark."

"Indeed it was. Had it not been for Soames to amuse me, I daresay I would have lost my mind much sooner."

"That caper merchant! And a mere boy, to boot." He had been jealous as sin of Soames from the moment he had met him, maybe sooner. He was very handsome and elegant.

"I am two years younger than Soames. Not quite an old hag yet myself." I had passed my twenty-third birthday while without memory.

"I noticed that detail right from the beginning, Rose," he said, arising from his chair and joining me on the sofa, where I was taking in his jacket. I had made him lose ten pounds. "Even in blue bombazine you were not quite an old woman."

I wore, at the time, a blue taffeta gown, cut low off the shoulders and with the Kessler sapphires around my neck, for we were dressed for dinner. I made the family dress properly for dinner every evening, and frequently displeased my husband by inviting company as well. We were dining alone on this particular evening, however. "Now you shall look less like an old man, with your jackets fitting your new trim figure."

"I wonder what gave you the notion you could be happy with an old man," he asked, hinting for some praise.

"It was living with Mr. Knightsbridge that led me to find you not quite ancient."

"I want you to have another small bout of memory loss to obliterate that part of your past, Beth."

"Just give me a tap on the head, a very slight one. Not too hard or I'll forget you, too."

"Annie likes a good big bump," he said, hefting a heavy brass box that held bonbons for her. I hadn't quite cured her of consuming a pound of sweets a day, but I made her eat meat at the table.

I readied my needle to defend myself, but he only opened the box and popped a candy into my mouth. "I don't want that," I complained.

"Hush, woman. Can't you see I'm trying to shut you up so I can kiss you?"

"No, you're trying to turn me into a big fat Rubens nude."

"A plain scrawny English nude is good enough for me."

"Lud! Abbie and Annie will be coming down any minute," I pointed out, as he set aside my needle and his jacket, with a lecherous light in his eye.

"That's why I'm in a hurry," he answered reasonably. He didn't seem to be in a hurry once he got started. It was a lengthy embrace that would better have waited till we were sure of privacy.

"I'm not really very hungry yet, are you? We could put off dinner . . ."

"Yes, I'm starved."

"Dinner isn't for half an hour."

"I guess I can wait that long."

"I can't." He arose and pulled me from the chair, out the door to the staircase. If you don't humor a German he can turn quite violent, so I went along quietly.

ABOUT THE AUTHOR

Joan Smith was born in Brockville, a small town on the St. Lawrence River, in Ontario. After finishing high school there, she attended Queen's University in Kingston and Teacher's College in Toronto. She taught English and French in high school, and English at college. She is married and has three children. Joan Smith began writing five or six years ago, her first efforts being gothic mysteries, which she still likes very much. Since then, she has written about 25 Regencies. She is an avid amateur gardener, reader of novels and social histories and art lover. Her plans for the future include owning a greenhouse and taking a trip around the world, and, of course, writing more books.

Let COVENTRY Give You
A Little Old-Fashioned Romance

THE LAST COTILLION   50078 $1.75
by Georgina Grey

BETH   50079 $1.75
by Barbara Hazard

NO IMPEDIMENT   50080 $1.75
by Mira Stables

SIR RANULF AND THE RUNAWAY 50081 $1.75
by Audrey Blanshard

LETTY BARLOW   50082 $1.75
by Joan Mellows

JESSICA   50083 $1.75
by Sandra Wilson

Let COVENTRY Give You
A Little Old-Fashioned Romance

MARY, SWEET MARY   50094 $1.75
by Claudette Williams

A CLANDESTINE AFFAIR   50095 $1.75
by Sally James

CHRISTINA   50096 $1.75
by Caroline Arnett

MINUET   50097 $1.75
by Jennie Gallant

DAPHNE   50098 $1.75
by Sarah Carlisle

THE COUNTERFEIT BRIDE   50099 $1.75
by Vivian Connolly

Buy them at your local bookstore or use this handy coupon for ordering.

This offer expires 1 June 81   8057

A NEW DECADE OF
CREST BESTSELLERS

THE LAST ENCHANTMENT *Mary Stewart*	24207	$2.95
CENTENNIAL *James A. Michener*	23494	$2.95
THE COUP *John Updike*	24259	$2.95
METROPOLITAN LIFE *Fran Lebowitz*	24169	$2.25
THE RISE AND FALL OF THE THIRD REICH		
William Shirer	23442	$2.95
THURSDAY THE RABBI WALKED OUT		
Harry Kemelman	24070	$2.25
IN MY FATHER'S COURT		
Isaac Bashevis Singer	24074	$2.50
PRELUDE TO TERROR *Helen MacInnes*	24034	$2.50
A WALK ACROSS AMERICA *Peter Jenkins*	24277	$2.75
WANTED! THE SEARCH FOR NAZIS IN		
AMERICA *Howard Blum*	23409	$1.95
WANDERINGS *Chaim Potok*	24270	$3.95
DRESS GRAY *Lucian K. Truscott IV*	24158	$2.75
THE GLASS FLAME *Phyllis A. Whitney*	24130	$2.25
THE SPRING OF THE TIGER *Victoria Holt*	24297	$2.75
TYPE A BEHAVIOR & YOUR HEART		
Friedman, M.D. & Rosenman, M.D.	23870	$2.50

Buy them at your local bookstore or use this handy coupon for ordering.

COLUMBIA BOOK SERVICE (a CBS Publications Co.)
32275 Mally Road, P.O. Box FB, Madison Heights, MI 48071

Please send me the books I have checked above. Orders for less than 5 books must include 75¢ for the first book and 25¢ for each additional book to cover postage and handling. Orders for 5 books or more postage is FREE. Send check or money order only.

Cost $_____   Name _____

Sales tax*_____   Address _____

Postage_____   City _____

Total $_____   State _____ Zip _____

* *The government requires us to collect sales tax in all states except
AK, DE, MT, NH and OR.*

This offer expires 1 June 81   8051